GW01066167

Fox Blood

Moon Marked, Volume 3

Aimee Easterling

Published by Wetknee Books, 2018.

FOX BLOOD

First edition. December 23, 2018.

Copyright © 2018 Aimee Easterling.

ISBN: 978-1791983079

Written by Aimee Easterling.

Chapter 1

"I think this is called the walk of shame," Kira suggested, her voice cutting through the foggy evening air like a sword through warm butter. I swiveled in unconscious reaction, peering through almost-raindrops hovering around us on every side.

Between the fog and the night, I couldn't see anything, unfortunately. Which didn't mean we were alone...just that visibility was painfully low. Unfriendly werewolves could be hovering just out of scent range, waiting for the perfect moment to pounce upon us. Good thing I wasn't as oblivious as my pampered younger sister to the danger we were currently walking through.

So—"Shh," I huffed out, hoisting a trio of cardboard containers a little higher in my arms while hoping the suddenly overwhelming aroma of stale beer wasn't emanating from one of them. Perhaps I should have sprung for new boxes rather than begging for used ones behind the neighborhood liquor store....

"Well, it is, isn't it?" Kira demanded, turning around to walk backwards down the gravel road leading up to our secluded cottage. "I mean, if we weren't ashamed, we would've taken Gunner up on his offer to rent a moving truck. We would have come when it was daylight out. And we wouldn't have parked

1

twenty miles away so nobody would hear Old Red squeak her way up the drive."

"Old Red isn't so bad," I rebutted, defending the new-to-me car. I'd never wanted a vehicle until I began living over a hundred miles away from a boyfriend who only visited in the company of needy pack mates. Skype had kept us in contact, but I had needs that weren't being met via video chat.

Gunner had offered to throw money at the problem, but I wasn't ready for that level of entanglement just yet. So I'd found a new job, had saved my pennies, and had bought a twenty-year-old, off-brand vehicle the previous week.

Old Red made it feasible to move into a secluded, rural village without feeling like I was trapping myself and Kira next door to a bunch of werewolves. The car gave me an easy out if we needed to flee and allowed me to spend time with Gunner without having to become monetarily indebted to him. Now, however, I was having second thoughts about the cleverness of my ploy.

Because my skin prickled with warning of hidden werewolves in the vicinity. Turning in a tight circle, I barely managed to keep Kira's box of stage-magic paraphernalia from teetering off the top of the stack while I peered around the barrier. I *knew* they were out there. This was Atwood clan central after all. Even at the crack of dawn, there should have been patrollers out guarding the boundaries and early risers jogging down tree-lined paths.

Instead, the territory appeared empty even though it smelled far too strongly of wolf...plus impatient little sister. "And we didn't park twenty miles away," I continued, trying to get Kira off topic before I was forced to tell her what a walk of shame really was. "We parked a quarter of a mile away so Old Red's brakes wouldn't wake up the neighbors. It's the considerate thing to do. You need to learn to be polite now that we're denning with—"

"Whatever," Kira cut me off, darting away to dance up cobblestone steps toward our cottage. The first dead leaves of autumn lay on the stones between us, and in daylight I suspected they would have glowed beautifully orange or red.

In the evening fog, however, the discarded plant matter merely appeared gray, slippery, and dangerous...like everything else about this place.

"Kira, wait." I wasn't in fox form, so I couldn't be certain. But I got the distinct impression someone had marked his territory on the bottom step in the form of very lupine-smelling pee. Gunner had promised the pack was ready to welcome us into their midst, but urine wasn't generally considered a sign of open-armed acceptance. More worrisome, however, was the fact that the liquid had been deposited so recently that it still puddled atop the cobblestones in my path....

"*Kira.*" This time I snapped out her name as close as I could come to a werewolf compulsion. But, of course, we weren't wolves and my sister saw no reason to obey me.

Instead, she turned the knob of our new domicile without even glancing backwards. Pushed the door open into darkness...and walked straight through an overwhelming cascade of strangely sulfurous eau de wolf.

THE BOXES WERE ON THE ground and my sword was clasped in white-knuckled fingers before several sets of hands—at least they were furless—yanked my sister into the death trap. But I was four steps too slow to prevent them from enfolding her into their midst.

Enfolding her...and flipping on the light switch to reveal smiling faces and party banners. Apparently my attempt to move in after sunset hadn't been as secretive as I'd initially supposed.

"Surprise!" werewolves howled, only some of the voices human. Then a whoosh of displaced air warned me of Gunner's presence half a second before a large hand tucked itself into the small of my back. He guided me through the doorway, my sword reluctantly dissolving into the magical ether even as I did my best to paste a pleased smile onto my face.

"I take it surprise parties aren't your favorite," Gunner huffed into my ear while his free hand massaged tension out of my neck muscles. And even though I was bound and determined to give Gunner every opportunity to rebuild his splintered pack without our relationship derailing his efforts, I still found myself swiveling so his guiding arm turned into half of a hug.

"No, I'm not generally a fan of surprise parties," I agreed. "But I *am* glad to see you." After all, it had been nearly three weeks since we'd spent more than five minutes in close proximity. No wonder his fingers on my bare skin acted like balm. I melted into his arms, forgetting my worries as I tilted my head back in preparation for a kiss.

Only, no kiss was forthcoming. Instead, Gunner released me and pulled a small notebook out of one pocket.

"I'll be sure to remember that in case it comes up later," he said. And even though cold air where warm hands used to be explained the sudden rise of goosebumps along my exposed forearms, my shiver was out of proportion to the chilliness of the night.

Blinking slowly to tamp down my frustration, I stood up on tiptoes to peer at Gunner's notebook. And what he'd written returned the smile to my face. *"My place tonight once Kira's sleeping?"*

No wonder he hadn't wanted to even whisper the words in the midst of the pack where shifter ears were bound to overhear him. My cheeks heated even as my head snapped up to peruse the partygoers. Somehow I was positive every werewolf present had read Gunner's words right alongside me....

But the crowd looked just like it had previously. Werewolves partying. Werewolves laughing. Werewolves muttering in dark corners about the kitsunes in their midst.

"Maybe," I answered, trying to decide whether I trusted Atwood shifters enough to leave Kira alone in the cottage after night fell.

"Oh, that reminds me," Gunner interrupted, raising his voice until it was loud enough to be heard at the far end of the overcrowded living room. "New rule—all disputes must be settled with blades hereafter. Tournament rules, to first blood." Then, as someone near us complained that he knew nothing about blades, that swords were archaic. "If you need instruction, I recommend asking our new sword master for tips."

Gunner's hand settled against the small of my back, subtly pushing me forward. And once every eye was upon me—exactly what I'd hoped to avoid by taking the walk of shame with my sister—the pack leader added: "Don't forget to pay her. Old Red needs new brakes."

Then just like that, Gunner left me alone in a room full of werewolves with nowhere to hide and no choice but to follow him deeper in.

Chapter 2

"**H**e's besotted with you."

The voice curling over my left shoulder sounded pleasant, but it wasn't. Instead, my instincts screamed "*Angry werewolf behind you. Careful!*" one second before I swiveled around with a fake smile pasted on my lips.

"Edward. Left your posse behind, did you? Braving the scary kitsune all on your lonesome?"

Because the middle-aged male who'd been Gunner's principal ally in the battle against Liam was apparently not my greatest supporter. Moments earlier, Edward had stood at the center of the huddle of unhappy shifters shooting angry glances in my direction. So the fact he'd come all the way across the room to engage me likely meant he had an ultimatum to drop on my head.

Meanwhile, the rotten-egg aroma that permeated my cottage was so strong now I could only conclude it emanated from this shifter. It couldn't have been his signature aroma, however, or someone would have warned me about the foul stench.

"Bad choice of cologne," I noted even as he grabbed my arm and drew me into the dimly lit hallway with a grasp so bruising I had to fight down a flinch.

"This pack is barely hanging together," Edward growled as soon as we were out of easy earshot of the rest of the partygoers, not bothering to comment on my snarkiness about his scent. "Liam was important to us and now he's gone. Ransom was an asshole, but the transition away from him is still difficult. We don't need you here making things more complicated. If you love Gunner, you'll leave him alone."

I wanted to snipe right back...but, unfortunately, Edward hadn't said anything I didn't already believe to be truthful. On the other hand—"Gunner asked me to come here. So I came."

As I spoke, I stared at the hand clenched around my arm until Edward realized what would happen if his pack leader saw the lines of parallel bruises welling up beneath his fingers. Reddening, he shrank back so rapidly I might as well have swiped at him with my sword.

"Shit," the male muttered under his breath. "If he smells me on you, he'll go berserk."

This, at least, I was prepared for. Reaching into my pocket, I pulled out an aerosol can of scent-reducing compound, spraying it liberally across my injured flesh.

"I'm not here to make your life difficult," I said as I worked, the chemical drifting up my nose in the process so I had to pause and stifle a sneeze before I could go on. But then I returned to the most important business—clarifying my place within the Atwood pack. "I'm here to support Gunner," I continued. "And if you care about the clan, you'll let me get on with my task."

Which was all very true even though the words sat between us like a lump of brussel sprouts on the plate of a picky toddler. If Edward wanted the Atwood clan to hang together, he'd make nice and pretend he didn't have a bone to pick with the pack leader's mate.

I could tell from his scent—no longer quite so harsh and astringent—that Edward had gotten the message. Unfortunately, werewolves have a hard time dropping a juicy bone. "What happened four months ago..."

"Was the fault of an Atwood werewolf," I interjected, not wanting to remember the awful battle of wolf against wolf fueled by the kitsune magic of my dead mother. "I would never do anything to damage this pack."

The vigor of belief added volume to what was meant to be a private conversation, and this time I really did wince as my words rang a little too loudly in the echoing hall. *Shit.* I'd intended to say my piece to Edward then let him propagate it through the pack at the speed of werewolf gossip. I hadn't intended to create a scene.

Ignoring the shifter beside me, I swiveled just as I'd done while walking up the path with Kira. Unfortunately, this time I wasn't lucky enough to find our surroundings devoid of life. Instead, a tall, broad-shouldered werewolf towered in the open doorway between hallway and living room, silhouetted against the light behind his back.

"Something the matter?" Gunner demanded, taking in our proximity, our stiff-legged anger, the strange floral overlay of the de-scenting compound.

"Of course not," I lied. "Edward was just giving me the recipe for his famous lasagna."

Grimacing in what was clearly meant to be a smile, the male in question played along. "The secret," he offered, "is in the sauce."

"Hmm," Gunner started, far from satisfied. Only he had no time to debrief us further, because the living room behind him erupted into howls, growls, and one long, quavering scream.

"KIRA." THE WORD EMERGED from both my and Gunner's lips in perfect synchrony, but we didn't have time to gaze meaningfully into each other's eyes. Instead, I sprinted down the hallway, sword materializing in my hand in a blaze of blue-tinted glory even as Gunner rounded the corner three steps faster and dove into the melee of angry wolves.

Because, despite their alpha's ultimatum moments earlier, two-thirds of the pack had donned their fur forms and turned their teeth into weapons the second they felt threatened. Those still human were more obedient but no less dangerous—they'd grabbed up cutlery, some of it as long as my forearm.

Meanwhile, the entire room smelled like a forgotten egg factory, the scent even worse here than it had been beside Edward in the hall. *How did everyone manage to go against a direct order from their pack leader? Did Gunner forget to imbue his words with alpha compulsion?* The questions hovered over me like a foul-smelling storm cloud. But I pushed premonitions aside, hunting for my sister instead.

There she was...then there she wasn't as she shivered down into the red fur of her fox. Ever since Kira had melded with our mother's star ball, she'd been unruly and snarky and prone to shifting at the drop of a hat. Which wasn't helpful in the current situation...but the chain of events also meant that her unusual fur form hadn't been what set the werewolves off.

So what...?

I waited only long enough to glimpse Tank—Gunner's trusted second—tackling my sister and enfolding her in a were-wolf burrito of protection before I thrust my way deeper into the crowd away from them. Because the growling mob wasn't facing toward either me or Kira. Instead, they were pushing and shoving, trying to get into the kitchen, or perhaps through that to the dining room beyond.

Mindful of the fact that these were supposedly my pack mates, I used my elbows and knees rather than my weapon to open up a pathway. But it was slow going, teeth snapping and claws scraping as I pressed past. My favorite pair of jeans was going to be spaghetti by the time this was over...but on the plus side, Gunner would never know that Edward had been the one to leave a bruise on my upper arm.

With that heartening thought at the forefront, I thunked a werewolf on the nose with my sword hilt, taking advantage of the resulting pocket of space to press through the narrow door-way separating kitchen from living room. And my grin of triumph promptly faltered as I took in the scene on the other side.

Because there was a fox perched atop the stainless steel re-frigerator. Its fur was puffed up like the pelt of a cornered cat while its body pressed back against the wall behind it. No won-der since a werewolf currently swiped toward it with human fingers, attempting to pull the stranger loose from its hiding place.

There were a dozen other werewolves in the room with a similar agenda. But I had interest only in the much smaller ca-nine cowering above their heads. Because even though its fur was pitch black instead of blazing red like mine and my sister's, I knew the moment our eyes made contact that this wasn't any

mere fox wandered in out of the forest who'd accidentally ended up in my new home.

No, this was a kitsune. A being the like of which I'd never
met outside my own family. After all, what right-minded wild
animal would willingly walk into a cottage full of wolves?

Chapter 3

N *ot such smart behavior for a kitsune either*, I noted even as I continued elbowing my way closer to the refrigerator on which our uninvited visitor perched. Despite my snarky internal commentary, however, I was as in awe of this being as if it was a unicorn walking out of a rainbow and into my life.

Because I'd never met a kitsune who wasn't a direct relative. Could count the number of fox shifters I'd come in contact with on two fingers of one hand. If I'd thought about it, I would have realized that my mother had to emerge from somewhere. And yet, I'd somehow just assumed that Kira and I were the last of our kind.

"Who are you?" I murmured, knowing my words wouldn't carry over the yipping and snapping of the werewolves between us. But, somehow, the fox heard. Swiveled its ears. Gently inclined its head.

There was a spark in the center of the being's eyes that made me stretch forward to lean in closer. And my existence must have been equally attractive to the midnight-furred animal. Because it crept toward me in perfect synchrony, still crouching low enough to protect its belly even as it strove to capture a better view of me.

Not it—she. After all, we were the same in every way that mattered. Never mind that I was two-legged while she walked on four paws. Never mind that her fur was black while mine was red. This was someone who would understand my deepest yearnings. This was another kitsune just like myself.

The tiniest hint of a whine emerged from the black fox's muzzle, her eyes watery with trust and request. Could I help her escape these werewolves...?

And in that moment of inattention, the shifters between us struck. One minute they were pushing and shoving, trying to reach the fox on human tiptoes. The next, a two-legger had boosted a four-legger on top of the refrigerator, placing the kitsune's ability to nod at me ever again into doubt.

Luckily, fridges aren't made for werewolf perching; the tops are too small and slippery for claws to find traction of any sort. And while the wolf teetered, unable to snap up its prey while maintaining its own balance, I made a decision that I knew I'd later regret.

"Here!" I called to the black fox, letting my sword recede as I stretched out both arms toward her. "Jump! I'll protect you!"

Because I couldn't let an innocent being perish, even if the last thing this pack needed was two kitsunes facing off against a mob of angry werewolves.

And the fox trusted me. Leapt across the surging, seething shifters who separated us to settle into my arms as easily as Kira had done hundreds of times during our thirteen-year shared past. Only, unlike my little sister, the stranger tucked her paws inward to ensure she didn't scratch me. And her eyes, when they met mine, were full of gratitude rather than snark.

The lump in my throat came from instant bonding. My arms tightened, my shoulders hunching over to protect the black-furred critter I hugged into my chest. I inhaled the soft musk of fox fur…and in that moment of calm and quiet, the wolves forgot I was Gunner's and launched themselves at me en masse.

"Get out!"

Gunner's roar was so loud it rattled the windows. Or maybe that reverberation was due to the thunder of a hundred feet as werewolves fled in the face of their pack leader's wrath. Whatever the reason, I was no longer in danger of losing my throat to supposed pack mates and my nose was grateful for the abrupt cessation of sulfur. So I uncurled from around the black-furred kitsune and peered up at my rescuer…who held a very naked yet very human Kira against his chest.

The alpha's arm was steely without denting my sister's skin painfully. And at the same time he still managed to look so murderous he might have stopped his underlings' breath with a single command. In reaction, the black fox nestled closer into my body, clearly terrified of the aura of electricity emanating from the wolf blocking her ability to retreat.

The fox's fear I would deal with in a minute. For now, I rose while scanning Kira's exposed limbs. "Are you okay?" I asked.

"Not that you care," my sister answered, brows lowering. "I might have been dead. I might have been injured. And you ran off in the opposite direction without even bothering to check on me."

"I'm checking now." And I'd also seen both Tank and Gunner racing directly toward my sister, so I'd known she was better protected than anyone else in the house.

Still, the pout on Kira's face promised she wouldn't let me off the hook so easily. Meanwhile, my quick survey of her limbs proved that the werewolves in question had done their job quite well. So I sighed acceptance of the fact that I was currently incapable of pleasing my sister and returned my focus to the strange fox instead.

Was Gunner really willing to fold yet another kitsune into his faltering clan structure? And would the pack splinter further if I dared to ask?

"Gunner..." I started, not sure exactly how to explain the fact that I ached to help this black-furred kitsune. It wasn't so much a humanitarian mission as a compulsion and a *need* as imperative as hunger.

But apparently explanations were unimportant. Because the skin around his eyes crinkled ever so slightly as he jerked his chin upwards in a promise. As long as I didn't sneak off on my lonesome, this werewolf had my back.

So—"You can shift," I told the fox, prying her away from my neck and placing her on the kitchen table beside me, the separation hitting me in the gut for just a second before it eased. "Gunner won't hurt you. I promise. We'll protect you from whatever drove you here."

Of course, the kitsune didn't regain her human form immediately. Instead, her dark eyes flickered back and forth between me and Gunner. She was assessing, gauging, calculating her chances....

In response, the rest of us kept our bodies relaxed and our gazes averted. And even though our body language was more lupine than vulpine, the black fox still gave a tiny whine of ac-

ceptance before shimmering into the form of a naked, redheaded girl.

"I'm Oyo," she whispered, gaze trained on the floorboards
as her legs beat against the side of the table she sat atop. She was
younger than me but older than Kira. In human terms, I would
have guessed she was just barely old enough to drink.

"My mate speaks for me," Gunner answered formally. "Just
as she's promised, so do I promise. Tell us who's chasing you
and we'll make sure they never find you again."

His words were protective, exactly what you'd expect from
an alpha werewolf. But his tone was still gravelly with rage from
the preceding battle, and his fur-form self was almost visible as
he took one step toward the girl.

No wonder Oyo didn't realize his advance was an offer to
guard rather than a threat of imminent danger. Squeaking in
reaction to the vague menace, the redhead was a redhead no
longer. Instead, she'd fallen back down into the skin of her fox.

Chapter 4

O yo scurried for cover, disappearing behind the refrigerator. Gunner growled in frustration then pulled me in the opposite direction even as he barked orders at his most trusted underlings, who had braved his wrath by remaining in my disaster zone of a living room.

"Allen, I want to know why no one smelled or saw a stray kitsune walking into clan central under her own power. Tank, check the perimeter and figure out where she came in."

His gaze slid across me so fiercely that I found words tumbling out of my mouth before I could consider whether they helped or hurt matters. "Gunner, I didn't invite..." I started, his sudden burst of alpha highhandedness making me wish my fingers were wrapped around a sword hilt rather than stuck in his crushing handhold.

"Edward, the pack needs reassurance," Gunner continued as if I hadn't spoken. "Think of a solution *now*." Then, as the last few werewolves waiting in the living room scattered, he turned to face me at last. "Yes, Mai, I know you didn't invite her." The statement seemed to absolve me of all wrongdoing, but his harsh tone didn't quite match his words.

And even though I knew Gunner was on edge from the recent risk to me and Kira, annoyance nonetheless flared at being treated like a toddler's doll. Because every time the alpha turned one way, I was dragged along behind him. Then he'd swivel in the opposite direction and give me a severe case of whiplash.

"I'm not..." I started, not quite sure what I wasn't. But this time the high-handed alpha hushed me with a finger to my lips even as he yanked out his phone and tapped rapidly at the screen.

"Brother, what a surprise." The call went through after only one ring, Ransom's voice so saccharine that it made my teeth ache. Or maybe that was just my fox incisors pushing their way through human dentition and gums in an effort to get out.

Either way, I wished I could see the elder Atwood's face through the cell phone. Had he answered so quickly because he'd sent Oyo to disrupt clan central? Or had he simply been at loose ends and thought baiting his brother might be a good way to fill an otherwise quiet night?

If I'd been the one in charge, I would have danced around the matter in an effort to tempt Ransom into dropping private information. But Gunner wasn't human enough for small talk, at the moment. Instead, he merely demanded, "Who did you tell?"

The words were a mistake—all three of us understood that as soon as they were uttered. And the smugness in Ransom's silence spurred me to take matters into my own hands in an effort at damage control.

"Ransom, thank you for accepting our call," I interjected, pressing my face closer to the phone and half expecting Gunner to yank the device away from me even as I spoke. But he didn't. Instead, he closed his eyes then swiped one huge palm across his face as if to remove overwhelming frustration. And when his sienna eyes blinked back open, they were full of both apology and praise.

Taking that as my cue to continue, I offered Ransom a sliver of information, hoping he'd give us something back in exchange. "A strange fox shifter showed up here this evening, which has your brother understandably excited. What he meant to ask was—do you have any idea how a kitsune might have heard this would be a safe place to hide?"

That conundrum had been roiling through my head ever since Oyo appeared on top of my refrigerator. After all, Gunner had kept my and Kira's identity so closely under wraps that only our pack and Ransom's should have known there were any kitsunes still living. So how had a stray fox shifter known to sneak into my home?

But apparently Oyo wasn't the biggest issue for the pair of siblings. Instead, Ransom's reply was clearly aimed not at me but rather at his brother.

"Who did I tell about you harboring illegal kitsunes? Is that what you meant to ask me?" Then, without waiting for confirmation: "No one yet, brother. But just imagine what might happen if I did."

"I SHOULDN'T HAVE TOLD him about Oyo."

I was kicking myself for playing right into Ransom's hands. But—despite the cell phone shattered on the ground and the strong scent of fur hovering around us—Gunner was back in control of himself and didn't appear to blame me.

No, it was his brother who served as the focus of the pack leader's ire. "He was lying," Gunner grumbled as he paced back and forth through the living room, crunching shattered glass and crockery beneath his boots.

"Maybe not," I interjected from my spot perched atop the arm of a blue, plush sofa. "Maybe I just gave Ransom an opening to threaten you. I'd be more certain he was responsible if you hadn't been the one to call him first."

Unfortunately, rational cause and effect clearly weren't working yet inside my favorite alpha's noggin. Because he kept walking and talking as if he hadn't heard my words at all. "If Ransom is spreading the word that you and your sister are under my protection," he growled, "then everyone knows he and I are no longer an unbeatable alliance. Our pack didn't have to fend off vultures when our father died because Ransom and I were united in our defense of clan central. But with only me on the job...we should start expecting visits from neighboring packs."

"Visits?" That didn't sound horrible. But from Gunner's tone, I had a feeling these neighbors weren't the welcome-wagon sort of werewolves. Sure enough, he shook his head as he continued pacing. Then, abruptly, he pulled me to my feet and brushed one absurdly gentle hand across the top of my head.

"Please be a little more careful of your own skin," he murmured, warm breath brushing over my forehead. His voice was still gravelly, but the *please* made up for all of his former heavy-handedness, warming locations lower down than my heart.

"I will," I promised, leaning into his broad body. But before I made contact, before I could turn that opening into a moment of shared pleasure...Gunner had set me back down on my sofa arm and disappeared out the door.

Unfortunately, the larger problem didn't disappear along with him. Instead, once my libidinous haze lifted, I clearly heard Kira slamming around in the kitchen. Oyo was silent but presumably still hiding. And my phone beeped to herald the arrival of an incoming text.

Cringing at the appearance of a number I'd never seen before but that I suspected corresponded to Gunner's brother, I swiped a reluctant finger to open the message up.

"I grant you free passage to and from Kelleys Island if you'd like to come and talk about it."

And wasn't that just going to float Gunner's boat?

Chapter 5

While I was focusing on Ransom, Oyo must have found a better hiding place. Because she was no longer behind the refrigerator when Kira picked her way through a minefield of spilled cheese dip and broken crockery to reach my side.

"I'm starving," my sister noted.

"So eat," I replied, dismissing Oyo's absence—if I couldn't find the visiting kitsune, then likely the pack couldn't either—while turning Ransom's text over in my mind.

Was Gunner right in pointing the finger at his brother? Was Oyo's arrival merely bait intended to tempt neighboring packs into tearing Atwood clan central down?

"Maaaaiiiii. You don't care about me at aaaaaaaalllllll." Kira's whine was an eleven on the one-to-ten whine-o-meter. And even though I didn't want to encourage that behavior, one glance at paw prints on counters and glass shards peppering every edible item gave me an idea on how to keep her busy and allow me to reward good behavior at the same time.

"Help me clean up the worst of this mess and we'll go find a restaurant."

"Pancakes?" Kira's eyes lit up even as she half-heartedly opened a closet door in search of a dustpan.

"Whatever you want," I answered, hoping I wasn't making a promise I couldn't make good on. After all, it was getting late even for dinner. I wasn't so sure an all-day-breakfast joint would miraculously materialize within an easy drive.

But Old Red was outside, ready and waiting. And the agreement was enough to spur my sister into action. Starting in the kitchen, we swept and scrubbed and cleaned intensively enough for us both to grow filthy and sweaty, for Kira to turn cranky, and for me to wonder what I was doing moving in with this pack.

Because our neighbors were werewolves. They walked into each others' houses without knocking, knew everything there was to know about everybody else's business...and yet not a single neighbor had returned to the scene of the crime to help us deal with this horrifying mess.

"How much longer do we have to...?" Kira started. But I didn't need her whine to spur me into action this time.

"We're going," I interjected, deciding that both clutter and Oyo would be okay on their own for a little while longer. If the black-furred kitsune was savvy enough to have made her way through pack territory without being sniffed out, she could continue hiding in the cottage until we got back.

"Just give me five minutes to shower," I started, intending to finish with: *And then we'll find pancakes.* But as Kira pushed ahead of me into the living room—a disaster zone we hadn't even started to deal with—I froze, smelling the scent of fur so strongly that I knew a werewolf was right outside the open door.

Only, I was wrong. Because, with a yip, the cutest wolf pup imaginable jumped out from under the couch and dove into a bowlful of beef jerky.

There weren't werewolves outside stalking us. There was one very curious youngster right inside our home.

Inside our home and getting ready to chow down on food that was likely full of glass shards. "Kira, grab it!" I commanded, knowing I wouldn't be able to sidestep my sister's body in time to stop the pup myself.

And, for once, my sister obeyed without argument. She launched herself at the young werewolf, snagging its rear foot and dragging it toward her even as it wriggled in protest at losing access to its chosen feast.

"Calm down," she chided as she grabbed for the pup's ruff and ended up encircling its neck instead. The grip was meant to be protective but looked an awful lot like attempted murder....

No wonder a roar of rage preceded the arrival of a much larger animal into our midst. The werewolf in question leapt through the open doorway with eyes blazing, then she landed stiff-legged right in the middle of a spray of broken glass.

WHETHER OR NOT THE adult wolf cut her paws, none of us noticed. Because she was far more dangerous than the glass beneath her feet. The wolf took one look at Kira's stranglehold on the wriggling puppy, then she skidded across carpet in her haste to tear my sister apart.

"Hey! Over here!" I waved the sword that had materialized in my hand, doing my best to look both imposing and dangerous. Not that I planned to slice open a mother protecting her child. But I also refused to let my own sister be injured due to an overprotective parent's wrath.

And the sword did the job I'd intended—it focused the adult wolf's attention quite firmly on me rather than on my sister. Swiveling, the female bared her teeth in momentary warning, then she lunged directly at me.

Dodging wasn't an option when my opponent was traveling so quickly. Meanwhile, behind my back, Kira emitted a terrified squeak. So I did the only thing I could think of. I softened my sword magic until it became immaterial, then I hardened it again into the form of a club.

Thwack! My edgeless weapon struck the wolf's shoulder so hard she tumbled forward into a summersault, but she was back on her feet before I'd regathered my own momentum and put up my guard. This time, her paws struck my shoulders and I was the one falling backward, something sharp slicing through the side of my left arm as I tried—and failed—to make my escape.

"No teeth!" Kira roared, her words sounding distant as the wolf's hot breath licked against my cheek, my chin, then lower. I struggled to turn my magic into a shield to protect my jugular, but I couldn't seem to regather either my powers or my wind.

I couldn't believe I'd lost to a mother wolf protecting her child. I couldn't believe....

Then we both shuddered in tandem as Kira slammed a fist into the wolf's belly. "Your *alpha*"—punch, pant—"said to fight with swords *only*"—kick, twist—"so what kind of pack wolf are you?"

Kira was magnificent above us, and she also brought up a very good question. Why was yet another Atwood shifter willing and able to disobey her pack leader's overt command? Perhaps I could chalk this up to maternal instinct, but after the melee surrounding Oyo I wasn't so sure.

The inconsistency felt important...but not quite as important as the claws digging into my skin. Then the pup was on top of me also, attracted by the blood of my oozing forearm. The youngster bared its teeth and started gnawing, and in reaction the female above me growled before shifting back into human form.

Becky. I remembered her name from our meeting last summer. Recalled the way she'd helped Gunner with transportation so he could hunt a bear and wrench the pack away from his brother without descending to the level of a physical fight.

Not that it had worked out as painlessly as we'd hoped after Becky tossed us those car keys. There'd been plenty of blood on the ground before the night was over, and Becky's mate had been one of the few who lost his life.

No wonder she'd been ready to tear me to pieces. But, to my surprise, the naked woman's face twisted apologetically as she scooped up the puppy, then she danced backwards rather than menacing me a second time.

"Curly, we do *not* gnaw on humans," she chastised, holding her offspring by his ruff and shaking him until he whimpered acknowledgement of the misunderstanding.

Then, turning back to me, Becky dropped her eyes to the floor even as that rotten-egg odor I was becoming unfortunately familiar with filled the room. "Alpha's mate. I was overwrought and out of line. I apologize for the misunderstanding. Please forgive me for the mistake."

Chapter 6

"Everything will be forgiven," I said simply, "if you tell me the fastest way to get pancakes into this starving teenager."

"The *fastest* way?" Becky's eyebrows rose and the sulfurous scent fled. "The fastest way is to go to the midnight breakfast Edward is organizing. But I'm not sure it's the smartest thing to...."

"Who cares about smart? I want pancakes," Kira interrupted, heading toward the door. "Midnight breakfast! I love being a wolf!"

And I *could* have stopped her forward motion. I probably should have too, given the way her usually sunny temperament seemed to be descending into demands and domineering at the drop of a hat. But, for once, Kira was smiling...and I was starting to get an idea of what caused the here-one-moment-gone-the-next scent of sulfur. So I didn't even interrupt my sister's chatterbox monologue as we strode along a secluded road and out into a well-lit picnic scene.

I was physically hungry, the salty tang of bacon dragging me toward the food being carried out in huge vats and on platters. And I was also hungry for companionship, glad to find the clan had forgotten us for a reason that didn't relate to the shape of our fur-form skins.

Still...Gunner must have known about this community mealtime and he hadn't dropped back by to invite me. Which suggested Becky was right and this wasn't the smartest place to feed my sister and my soul.

No wonder my eyes scanned our surroundings, looking out for signs of danger even as I noted the distinct lack of familiar faces in the werewolves' midst. Tank, Allen, and Gunner were all elsewhere, but at least there was no rotten-egg aroma filling the Green. Well, there wasn't until a gob of spittle struck the grass before us, a sulfur-scented werewolf I'd never met pressing her way into our personal space.

"Disgusting," the old woman growled, and I had my sword in hand to protect Kira before I realized the speaker wasn't interested in the two of us. Instead, Becky was the one scooping up her son, neck bent in submission. And Becky was the target of the old woman's jabbing finger as the crone continued with her tirade.

"If Old Chief Atwood was still alive, he never would have allowed such an abomination," the older woman said while spraying us all with spittle. "Liam knew better too. If he'd lived, he would have dealt with this rot before it went so deep."

She raised her cane as if to strike either Becky or Curly, which made me, in turn, prepare to tackle the foul-mouthed bitch. But clearly the call of pancakes was greater than the allure of ornery hatefulness. Or maybe the crone had finally noticed my aggressive stance. Either way, the old woman turned away with only a sniff of dismissal, taking her foul scent with her as she stepped into the longer of two lines forming up on either side of the expanse of grass.

I wanted to ask Becky what the deal was, but the female barely knew me and was unlikely to spill her guts in public. So, instead, I changed the subject. Heading toward the shorter line—the only one with bacon, were these werewolves crazy?—I offered, "Let's find ourselves something to eat."

"Not there." Becky's hand was on my arm then off again so quickly I barely registered the contact, and her gaze was still riveted on the ground as she spoke. But her voice was nonetheless loud enough for me to understand as she deciphered the bacon mystery for me. "That's the line for warriors. If you join it, you'll be asking for a fight."

Sure enough, a newly arrived family split up on the threshold. The father headed for the bacon, the mother and two children veered right toward pancakes and eggs. Rather than joining the end of the line, however, the male insinuated himself midway down it, setting the neighboring shifters bristling for a moment before they chose to subside. And, in reaction, the pancake line easily made room for the newcomer's family in the middle of the queue, right about where her mate would have stood had he chosen the longer line instead.

Seriously? Werewolves made even group meals into power struggles? Well, that answered the question about how to carve out a place for me and Kira within the Atwood community.

"I want scrambled eggs, pancakes, and a banana," I told my sister. Then, allowing my sword to form in its sheathe along my backbone, I headed for the bacon line.

GIVEN THAT GUNNER AND his closest lieutenants were apparently occupied elsewhere, I shouldn't have been surprised by the square shoulders and closely shorn hair at the head of the line. But as Edward turned around to face me and immediately emitted enough sulfur to drown out the delicious bacon aroma, I grumbled internally. Of course my least favorite Atwood werewolf would be the one I was facing to get my fair share of pig fat.

For half a second, I hesitated, considered choosing a spot a few werewolves back instead. Did I—and Becky and Kira by proxy—really need to proclaim ourselves the most dominant shifters in the entire clan? Wouldn't second or third best suffice just as well?

"Lost?" Edward asked as I debated. His smile was so smug as he motioned to the head of the opposite line that I felt my teeth grinding together even as the decision made itself. "The alpha's mate eats over there."

His words were a minor concession and everyone knew it. An acknowledgement that if Gunner were here, the pack leader would win by default and I'd head up the non-bacon-enabled queue.

But I didn't intend to hang upon Gunner's coattails. He had enough on his plate without slapping down shifters who disrespected me. Instead, I was perfectly willing to fight this battle on my own.

Willing...and excited as I drew my sword out of its sheathe with a musical ring of magic-imbued metal. I was sick and tired of backhanded put-downs. It was time for Edward to find a weapon and face me like a man.

Only, my chosen opponent had no intention of engaging in a sword fight. Instead, the male made room for me before him, somehow managing to turn a motion that should have been submissive into a slight instead. "By all means, if your only other option is to use a weapon none of us is familiar with. Stand in for Gunner. The rest of us will all move back."

There were grumbles from the queue behind me, high-pitched annoyance from the opposite side of the grass. Now I looked like a bully, unable to bend to Atwood customs and instead hiding behind Gunner's requirement that everyone in the pack settle their differences with swords.

That wasn't going to garner Becky the protection I was going for, nor would it smooth the path for my sister in the days ahead. So, opening my hands wide, I let my sword flare back into an immaterial star ball. Then, toeing out of my sneakers, I shifted into the form of my fox.

Chapter 7

"First blood, one-year moratorium on further fighting?"

The question came from behind me, the male second in line for bacon suggesting rules I understood to be the Atwood default in duels such as this. But Edward didn't answer, nor did he take the time to untie his shoelaces. Instead, he shifted in a burst of alpha aggression, shreds of fabric flying everywhere...including into the food trays we were all hoping to serve ourselves from.

Good thing I wasn't married to the idea of bacon, I noted even as I danced backward, assessing the shape of Edward's wolf. He was every bit as large as Gunner in fur form, his more advanced age far from obvious as he paced toward me on silent lupine feet.

Which would have been daunting eight months earlier. But I'd been sparring with the guys off and on all summer. I knew the relative strengths and weaknesses of fox form and was confident I could win first blood.

I was far less confident that I could vanquish my opponent if Edward declined to stop at a simple scratch and instead aimed for serious injury. But, in the skin of my animal, future worries quickly faded away. Instead, I yipped a playful taunt at the large canine facing me, then I slimmed down my body and scurried fast as an adder between his front legs.

Because male wolves were so blissfully predictable—get close to their reproductive organs and they transitioned from posturing warriors into terrified children in an instant. Edward was no exception. With a yelp, he plopped down on top of me, lying prostrate in an attempt to protect his family jewels from imminent attack.

Which solved the problem he was going for, but left his paw pads exposed, bare skin easy to scratch. Nipping hard with sharp fox teeth, I tasted salt exploding on my tongue.

First blood. Ten seconds after commencing our battle, I'd earned the right to stand at the head of the line.

Which should have been the end of the matter. Would have been if Edward had agreed to the other shifter's suggestion or if Gunner had been standing over us ready to growl the loser into defeat. As it was, however, my opponent wasn't thrilled at my not-quite-kosher victory. Or so I gathered as his snout darted toward me, teeth closing so hard around my ruff they nearly met in the middle despite the intervening fur and skin.

At least it was just a fold of pelt he was holding onto. He *could* have bitten straight through my neck and ended this entire game the easy way. But as I was slung back and forth so hard my eyeballs threatened to pop out of their sockets, I had a hard time feeling gratitude for anything at all.

Especially when Edward dropped me in front of another werewolf a few seconds later, this one in human form but with no less aggression in his grip as he used my ribs as a punching bag. I scratched as best I could, trying to escape or at least buy enough time to summon my star ball. But my magic was elusive and a fox was no match for a werewolf when the latter wasn't bound by the agreement of first blood.

And now I was being tossed to a third shifter. Then to another and another yet. As if no one wanted to hog the pleasure of proving the hard way that I didn't belong within their pack.

"Gunner won't answer his cell phone." Kira's voice sounded very far away as my head thudded against a shifter's foot this time. *Smart little sister to call for backup*, I thought vaguely even as I tried and failed to bring my magic to the fore once again. *Too bad she didn't realize Gunner crushed his phone underneath his boot.*

I was too confused to even attempt shifting to tell her that, though, and was starting to lose my ability to think. All I could muster was the knowledge that none of the preceding punches had cut through my skin or broken any bones. Which meant these shifters were, perhaps, hoping their alpha would never find out what had happened behind his back?

"The pack bond isn't working either." That was Becky. Or at least I thought it was Becky. I was starting to lose track of names...including my own.

Then my teeth contacted with the fist of yet another werewolf. And I *knew* the solution my addled brain hadn't been able to come up with before now.

I'd use kitsune magic to control these shifters. Would force them to release me. And, in the process, consolidate my place within the pack.

It was brilliant. Okay, maybe not so brilliant. But at least the strategy would ensure I made it out of this hazing alive.

I SHOULD HAVE POSSESSED a vast reservoir of available magic already since I'd bitten at least two of the werewolves in my efforts to escape from the beating. But my opponents had shaken that energy right out of me with their kicks and punches. Good thing I had more blood waiting to be swallowed...and with it access to the wills of every single shifter who had beaten me up until this point.

Because I'd fought back as best I was able while being manhandled. So little bits of werewolf matter were bound to be embedded beneath my claws. The only trick was reaching them, and doing so without biting off my own tongue in the process....

Even as I thought through a plan of action, my current manhandler tossed me skyward, probably intending to scare me but actually providing a much-needed reprieve. I almost scratched myself in the eye while attempting to lick the first toenail, but then dirty salt saturated my senses and hit me like a sugar rush right between the eyes.

Hold me over your head, I ordered the male who caught me as I descended. And I was pleased to find his two spread hands now formed a wide, raised platform rather than clenching back into menacing fists. Just what I needed—space and time to search for werewolf fluids while I was kept far out of other shifters' reach.

"Hey! What're you doing?"

"Come on! We weren't finished!"

The complaints grew louder and louder, but I ignored them as I licked and gnawed at my own nails. Then...

There. Heady energy flooded my senses, dulling the aches and pains that resulted from being pummeled so dramatically.

Now *I* was the powerful one. The one able to do whatever I wished with these werewolves. Time to see what my assailants thought of that.

Chapter 8

It was tempting to revenge myself upon the bullies. But now that my head was clearer, I understood that there was only one way to end this debacle. I had to rebuild the clan with me in the center rather than trying to fight my way inside.

Even as the thought coalesced into existence, visions emerged before my eyes. Glowing threads of connection slid hither and yon around me and I struggled to make sense of the images materializing beneath the magically obedient shifter's hands.

Could someone have kicked me in the head hard enough that I was hallucinating? I would have jumped to that conclusion quite willingly if the illuminated lines hadn't made far too much sense.

Because my own bonds were just what I would have expected. There was one connecting me with Kira, a slender thread leading to Becky, and several others flowing into the distance and out of sight.

The thickest led to Gunner. I somehow knew this without having to see the far terminus, knew this even though the scent of rose petals seemed to waft toward me down that particular bond.

What are you up to? I murmured, intrigued despite myself. And for half a second I looked out through the alpha's eyeballs.

Felt my/his fingers setting a bottle of bath salts on the edge of a massive tub even as wax melted from flickering candles arrayed all around the edge.

Aw. Gunner was setting the scene for our date this evening. Which was unbelievably sweet...and at the same time reminded me of what would happen if I called him here to save my skin.

The overprotective alpha would take one look at my bruises and go ballistic, a problem when pack bonds were already stretched and strained. After all, I could see Becky tugging hard on a thread that should have connected her to Gunner but was instead severed and faded. No wonder the alpha hadn't answered. He had no idea what was happening since Becky's connection was rotten and stinking five feet away from her hand.

The female wasn't the only one with that problem either. No, from up here werewolves looked like they were caught in an aged and decaying spider web. Even as I watched, more bonds snarled and splintered, each break setting off another burst of sulfurous scent.

Was this what my arrival had done to the pack that meant so much to Gunner? I was already regretting using kitsune powers to free myself since similar actions were likely responsible for the tangle we were all caught within.

But, on the plus side, watching Becky had filled me in on how pack bonds operated. So, tilting my head until my own tethers wrapped around my muzzle, I gave one of my lesser connections a tug.

ALLEN—GUNNER'S NERDY and level-headed lieutenant—didn't show up until I'd already shifted and started solving the problem the hard way. No, not with swords or punches but with much-needed TLC.

"It's over," I informed the watching shifters, trying to look like I wasn't analyzing them for signs of further attack...while covertly analyzing them for signs of further attack.

Because I'd relinquished magical control over their actions as soon as my feet hit the ground and my sword was back in my fist. Which left me wide open to the mob mentality, but I hoped also gave my audience an incentive to listen rather than react.

They glared at me but didn't argue, the sight of my injured body enough to give most of my recent assailants pause. Now that they weren't in the midst of their instinct-fueled blood haze, I could tell they'd started wondering what Gunner would do to them once he heard about the evening's events.

In the interest of returning their attention to what really mattered, I let them off the hook on that matter at least. "I'm not going to tell Gunner who hit me," I informed my audience. "I'll take a shower so he can't smell you. And if you're smart, you'll all wrestle or go for a run or do whatever werewolves do to get scratched up."

"Yeah, go sniff each others' butts," Kira snarked, not as quietly as she should have. My sister was going to be the death of me...and I had no solution other than to mouth, *"Go home."*

Luckily, Allen had been the right pack mate to summon. Because he took in my sister's orneriness and my precarious hold over the werewolves' attention in one split second of eye-squinting assessment. Then, snagging a relatively clean piece of bacon and a plateful of pancakes, he lured Kira away...while leaving Becky behind.

Okay, so Allen wasn't a perfect mind reader. Or maybe he knew that Kira was enough to keep his hands entirely full. So the older female would have to be part of my object lesson. But, first, I had to reel these werewolves the rest of the way in.

"Each of you needs to get over your snits," I continued, watching the rotted pack bonds with half my attention even as I met each shifter's eyes in turn. "For example—Edward, whatever you have against that pup beside you, you need to let it go."

Because the older shifter's bond to the nearby teenager looked like it had been shredded and gnawed on. Sure enough, both males' faces reddened as I called them on their relationship, then a young woman slapped Edward on the arm.

"Daddy, are you still mad at Chester from years ago?"

"He broke your heart. He doesn't deserve to be your mate."

"Sir—" the male in question started. But Edward's daughter spoke over him, standing up on her tiptoes so she could stare her father directly in the eyes.

"He had a small lapse when we were *children*," the young woman countered, and I had to admire her spirit even though I was pretty sure by my standards she hadn't grown out of being a child quite yet. "But it's over and done with, Daddy. You need to let the past stay in the past."

Old grudges don't heal in an instant. But I was relieved to note new tendrils of connection forming before I turned my gaze the other way. "Which brings me to another matter," I continued. I knew I was on a roll from the way each werewolf focused intently upon me—or maybe they were staring at the bacon behind my back.

No, they were buying what I was selling. "She can see the pack bonds clearly," one male murmured. "She *is* the alpha's mate," someone else quietly agreed.

"Yes, I am the alpha's mate," I continued. "And as such, I want to know what in the world you have against Becky and her son Curly?"

And, immediately, the virtual sunlight that had illuminated the gathering squelched into gathering storm. Brows lowered, shifters growled, and someone in the back shouted out a reply.

"That so-called *son* was born a bloodling with fur and wolf claws. If the old chief was still around to do something about it, that particular abomination would already be dead."

Chapter 9

S o *that* was why I hadn't seen any other tiny pups scampering through clan central. I took another look at Curly and realized that the youngster was probably less than a year old, his life apparently saved by the change of leadership that had occurred after Gunner's father died.

"Don't you think...?" I started, not sure how I was going to sway someone so mired in the past that he failed to realize a shifter in wolf form was still very much human. But before I could get my thoughts together, a woman around Becky's age darted out of the crowd and began screaming at the male who'd recently spoken.

"Oh, you'd like that, wouldn't you? To return to the Dark Ages? Not that we aren't there already. Who says I have to find a mate before I can enjoy bacon? Who do you think cooked all of the bacon in the first place? The women, that's who! And if we want to serve ourselves from the left line, we'll do that..."

"Mind your place, woman." It wasn't just the bloodling hater who was against this particular female, I realized. Watching the pack bonds with half my attention while trying not to sneeze against the rising tide of sulfur, I noted that fully a third of the males—including the current speaker—had withdrawn emotional support from the outspoken female the instant she began her harangue.

And there was nothing I could do about it. Nothing I could do but watch all of my good intentions crash and burn around me.

Because the magic that had gotten the pack's attention earlier was already slipping. My ability to yank on immaterial connections was dissipating even as the illuminated threads faded out of sight.

Unless I took another sip of werewolf blood, I had no way to stop this shouting match. And if I didn't calm agitated tempers, someone—like Curly—was bound to get hurt.

I turned around, searching the crowd for the young bloodling. And in the process I nearly ran into Becky, whose hand slipped into mine in order to urge me away.

"Let's go." She had Curly tucked under her other arm, a piece of bacon clenched in the pup's needle-sharp incisors. At least *someone* had profited from my misguided attempt to shake up the Atwood status quo.

Still—"I can't just leave them like this," I countered, struggling to come up with a solution that wouldn't make things worse in the long term. Gunner wasn't going to be pleased that I'd riled up the masses and left them to duke it out amongst themselves...just as he wasn't going to be pleased when he took a look at the bruises welling up all over my torso, legs, and arms.

Welling up...and aching the way they hadn't when they'd first been inflicted. I only realized the protective adrenaline was fading out of my bloodstream when I stumbled, leaning against Becky's shoulder in order to keep myself upright.

"You're in no position to stop them," Becky said, stating the obvious. "And...maybe it'll help to air all of our dirty laundry in public. It's worth a shot."

It was worth a shot only because we had no alternative. But a smart warrior knows when to retreat so she can later rise up and return to the fight.

So—hating to give in without a resolution, but unable to think of a better alternative—I pulled Becky forward this time, leaving the werewolves behind us to do their worst.

"YOU LOOK AWFUL."

I'd accepted Becky's offer to shower at her house, not really intending her to see the wounds her pack mates had inflicted upon me. But apparently she was as soft-footed as a fox. So she'd managed to sneak up on me as I stood in the bathroom, trying to decide whether my ripped and ruined clothing was worth putting anywhere other than in the trash.

"Here." She handed over an armful of clothing, apparently having thought of everything I hadn't. And even though I gladly slipped into the gifted underwear, I hesitated before pulling on the rest of her offerings.

Because my enemies hadn't just peppered me with bruises. In several places, my skin had split open, blood still oozing out and promising to ruin Becky's shirt and pants. Gunner wasn't just going to be disappointed. He was going to be furious. And what he did as a result would make my precarious position in the pack much, much worse.

I sank down onto the toilet lid, my knees suddenly refusing to hold me. In my mind's eye, I imagined the alpha waiting for me amid his bath salts and candles. He was trying so hard to make me welcome...and his efforts were tearing an already broken clan apart.

Kira and I should leave. The reality bit into my gut more painfully than any physical bruise or laceration. I needed to take myself away from this pack, but I didn't want to. Didn't want to lose not only my growing bond with Gunner but also the possibility of being part of something greater than I'd ever dreamed of involving myself in.

If I stayed, I'd no longer be a woman alone with her sister. I'd be a member of a pack.

But was it worth becoming part of a pack if that pack didn't want me? What if the pack in question was painfully misogynistic and actively dangerous to those I loved?

I knew the answer, much as I didn't want to. No wonder I barely registered Becky crouching down beside me and beginning to smear something green and gooey across my wounded skin.

"You know, Ransom's weaknesses and their father's ancient notions aren't the entirety of our pack's problem," she said tentatively, perhaps reading my mind or perhaps speaking from her own experience. "A werewolf leader needs to be mated. It sounds old-fashioned, but the female energy of an alpha's mate brings peacefulness to a clan."

"Yeah." I laughed despite myself. "I'm doing a really great job promoting peacefulness."

"You might be. In the long run. I at least appreciate what you've done for me." Her fingers were so skillful I didn't even realize I'd been plastered with bandaids until I looked down and saw a dozen pink stripes dotting my skin and hiding cuts and bruises. Tiny, rainbow-colored wolves danced and frolicked atop the plastic, and despite myself I barked out a curt but honest laugh.

I was cleaned up and bandaged...and somehow I'd decided not to flee into the night in the process. Or at least not into *this* night. I'd stick it out for one more day and see if there was a way to help rather than harm this pack.

But I couldn't deepen my bond to Gunner until I knew how long I was staying. So after hugging Becky in gratitude, I turned right instead of left out of my new friend's driveway.

After all, Kira needed someone to watch over her. Plus, I was exhausted and, apparently, cowardly. So rather than hunting down the alpha who had claimed me, I headed back to the cottage I had tentatively begun calling my own.

Chapter 10

Allen must have traded off with Tank sometime after dropping off my sister, because the latter nodded at me from his post beneath Kira's window as I headed back up the steps to the shadowed front door. So Kira would have been fine if I'd kept my word and gone to Gunner's as promised. Still...I wouldn't sleep until I was sure that both my charges hadn't been harmed while I was away.

So I padded through the living room and kitchen before giving in to the beckoning bedrooms. "Oyo?" I murmured into the darkness, rising on tiptoes to swipe a hand across the empty top of the refrigerator where the kitsune had first been found. The space was bare, unsurprisingly. After all, our guest was too smart to hole up anywhere so obvious. Still, various other nooks and crannies were equally unoccupied. So perhaps the missing female had gotten smart and snuggled up with Kira on her bed?

Retracing my footsteps through the living room, I turned right this time into the hallway that led to the two bedrooms beyond. And there I stopped as I caught sight of a lump on the floor in front of Kira's door. A body swaddled in blankets as if Oyo had been afraid to choose a bedroom and had instead made herself a pallet. It clenched my stomach to think of her sleeping on the floor.

"Oyo?" I whispered, not wanting to wake my sister but aware that a kitsune can be dangerous to startle in the darkness.

And the sleeper woke instantly, rising upwards while shedding blankets right and left. Only this wasn't Oyo. This was Gunner, shirtless and so handsome the vision stole my breath. "Our guest is hiding in the laundry room," he offered, making me frown for one split second as I considered the fact that I hadn't even realized my new home possessed a washer and dryer let alone a room to keep them in.

"Laundry nook," he corrected himself as he stood and took three long strides forward to meet me halfway down the hall. "Behind the folding doors off the kitchen."

Oh, right. I'd assumed that was a pantry and hadn't bothered to look inside it. Not a very comfortable spot to spend the night...but whatever made Oyo feel safe.

We were eye to eye now, and Gunner's proximity was sending messages to my battered body that I was hard-pressed to fight against. Leaning forward, I murmured, "Sorry I didn't show up for the bubble bath."

"I saw you had your hands full when you contacted me through the pack bond," Gunner answered, his own hands rising to rub firm circles of pleasure across shoulders that ached then soothed. "I figured I'd finish cleaning up your cottage since you were cleaning up my pack for me."

So he wasn't angry about the mob scene? I was glad...and also subtly disappointed. Maybe I'd gotten a little too used to an alpha werewolf's overprotective streak.

Perhaps that's why I didn't fill him in about the as-yet-unanswered text from his brother. Or perhaps it was the warm comfort of Gunner's fingers on my skin sidetracking me from that line of thinking. His hand slid beneath my shirt's collar, skimming lines of fire sideways across my upper chest while giving other parts of my body intriguing notions I was suddenly ready to act upon.

"Perhaps..." Gunner started.

Then his nail caught on a bandaid and his wolf emerged behind his eyes with a growl. "What exactly," the alpha demanded, forgetting to be quiet for the sake of my sleeping sister, "happened to you?"

"CALM DOWN."

Okay, so even I knew that was no way to start a conversation with an angry werewolf. Still, I was desperate to finish what we'd started. Desperate enough to tug Gunner back toward the pallet of blankets and muffle my own admonition by pressing lips against bare skin.

I kissed my way up his fingers, his arm, and onto his neck, the whole time trying to make myself believe that Gunner was still riding the same libidinous train I was. But his muscles were not only hard, they were unyielding. The discovery of my bandaids had thoroughly derailed us from the pleasure-seeking track.

Eventually, I settled back on my heels, accepting that Gunner's interest wasn't going to flick back on until we'd dealt with his outrage. And when he spoke, his voice was quieter but no less intense as he demanded the same information in a slightly different way.

"Who injured you?"

The hand I'd been kissing was still relaxed and open against my body. But his left fist, I noted, was so tightly clenched it was obvious that identifying my assailants would send Gunner rushing off to pound them into a pulp.

"You know it's inevitable that I'll get a little injured on occasion if I'm denning with werewolves," I started, forcing his fist back into the shape of a hand even as I let my dreams for the evening fade into the dark. My goal now was to keep Gunner from slaughtering his pack mates. Getting lucky would have to wait for another night.

"I'll kill them."

I was very glad now that I'd taken advantage of Becky's shower before running into Gunner. And also glad that, while hunting through the cottage for Oyo, I'd come up with a potential cure both for my contusions and for Gunner's over-protective rage.

So I reached over to tip his head down until our eyes met, then I offered a partial solution. "If you're willing, I think I can heal most of these wounds with a little turbocharge."

"Blood, you mean?" Gunner hesitated, his urge to annihilate my opponents battling with his ever-present need to keep me safe.

"If you're willing," I repeated. And I could see the moment his softer side won out over his bloodlust.

"We're not done talking about this," he told me. But then he used his mouth for something more useful, ripping a small cut at the crook of his elbow and offering up the wound so I could take a sip.

We hadn't shared blood in months, and the rightness of the experience was oddly arousing. My nipples tightened, my skin prickled, and I found myself smearing Gunner's fluids over his face as I moved my head upward to steal a kiss.

I thought he was right there with me, too, until a sting on my shoulder alerted me to the removal of one of my bandaids. Then Gunner drew away from my lips and pulled the collar of my shirt sideways so we could both peer underneath.

There was nothing to see but clear skin, unblemished and smooth as if I'd never been hit in the first place. Meanwhile, aching muscles soothed as if I was enjoying that promised bubble bath after all.

And even though I hadn't really done anything to make the healing happen, I could feel exhaustion cascading back over me. Which meant I was the one who shut down further shenanigans. I was the one who murmured a thank you even as I subsided back onto the blankets spread across the floor beneath us.

Still, I was awake enough to hear Gunner's answer. "Thank you for sacrificing yourself for the pack's problems," he rumbled. Then, intertwined in each other's arms, we fell deeply asleep.

Chapter 11

I woke to cold air, a solitary pallet, and my sister shrieking. "I've been stabbed!"

So Gunner had gone to deal with my assailants after all. And one of them must have snuck through our defenses to return the favor....

Those thoughts tumbled through my head as I wrenched the door open, only to find Kira standing on her bed in a tank top and undies, blood running down the insides of her thighs. She hadn't been stabbed. If I didn't miss my guess, she'd merely become a woman, starting her menstrual cycle for the very first time.

Which should have been my cue to commence mothering. But instead...I froze.

Froze and flashed back to my own first period. To hiding in the bathroom and clutching my belly while my father struggled to take care of an infant without letting us know he'd succumbed to grief at the death of his wife.

We'd been lost without my mother just as I was now lost calming Kira. Up until this point, I'd just mimicked Mama's parenting. But by the time I started my period, our own mother had been dead.

So I stood and Kira shrieked....and the window shattered behind her to disgorge a human-form werewolf. Tank had slivers of glass embedded in his skin from tumbling through the opening. But he did no more than brush free his hands before scooping my sister up off the bed.

"Who did it? Where are you injured?" He spun her around seeking a wound, and Kira let him manhandle her for a moment before looping her arms around his neck so she could sob into her protector's sweatshirt.

"It hurts," the teenager moaned. "And it's nasty." Meanwhile, Tank's search found the obvious source of the red fluid and the werewolf turned unaccountably pale.

Typical male reaction. I tried to laugh off Tank's weakness so I could step forward to take over care of my sister. But what was the right way to calm down a hysterical teenager whose fists were even now pounding a staccato rhythm on her protector's broad chest?

"What's wrong?" Dad had asked me twelve years earlier, after I slammed a plate onto the table so hard it shattered into sharp-edged shards.

"Nothing, nothing, nothing!" I'd howled, wanting to shift to fox form and bite him until he hurt as much as I did.

"Mai, honey. I know it's hard without your mother. But we're all in this together. You don't have to suffer alone."

His words hadn't actually helped me, but they *had* shamed me into silence. Which wasn't what I wanted—to squelch my sister's feelings. The trouble was, I couldn't recall what kind of reaction I'd actually been looking for when I was newly menstrual. I hadn't known then and I definitely didn't know now.

So once again I hesitated, frozen by difficult memories. And during that hiatus, someone pushed past me wrapped in a robe and smelling strongly of dryer sheets.

"Kira, stop it." Oyo gently tugged my sister away from the werewolf who actually *was* bleeding from various wounds still embedded with wicked glass shards. "It's just your period, honey," she continued, setting Kira down on the edge of the bed. "We'll clean you up and you'll be hunky dory again."

"You don't understand!" Kira countered, pounding her fists against Oyo's shoulder this time. If I didn't miss my guess, horror had turned the corner while we weren't looking and morphed into rage. "My body betrayed me! It's a disaster! I'll never be the same person I was yesterday."

"Get us some damp washcloths," Oyo told the hovering werewolf, giving Tank something helpful to do while he caught his breath. Then, drawing me forward with raised eyebrows, she grasped one hand from each of us, waiting until Kira and I had intertwined our other fingers and created a triangle of unity with my sister inside.

"You're right, Kira. You'll never be the same as you were yesterday," the formerly quiet kitsune continued. She no longer appeared small and scared, I noted. Instead, I leaned into the younger woman, trusting her implicitly. "You've joined the womanhood. It's sometimes painful, sometimes difficult. But it's always worth the blood."

And that was apparently the right thing to say after all. Because Kira raised our joined hands to swipe tears off her cheeks. "You promise?"

"I promise," Oyo answered.

"Mai?"

"It's worth it," I said honestly, remembering how shaken up I'd been by my first period but how glad I was to be a woman now.

Which wasn't at all what I would have told Kira if Oyo hadn't insinuated herself into the family drama. I likely would have gone all sex ed on her, providing a rundown on hygienic products along with a tart reminder that she could now become pregnant if she risked unprotected sex.

All of the hard data could wait for later, however. Instead, what Kira needed this morning was unconditional love and support.

So I squeezed two kitsunes' hands with warming fingers and growing gratitude. It was such a relief to take part in a ritual like Mama might have come up with. And right then and there, I decided that I'd find some way to keep everything. The pack, Gunner, and Oyo also.

Because even if the doing was painful and difficult, I had a feeling incorporating this stranger into my family would be well worth the blood.

Chapter 12

"Thank you," Oyo told me ten minutes later as I handed over a pair of jogging pants. She sounded so genuinely grateful for such a small gift that I paused in the act of rooting through my as-yet-to-be-unpacked boxes in search of a semi-matching shirt.

"Hey, I should be the one thanking you," I told her before delving deeper into the mess of fabric. "I had no idea what to tell Kira. You must have a big family to know exactly what to say."

"A big family?"

Right. Kitsunes didn't come from big families. Barring those who made a mistake with birth control and chose to sacrifice their own lives for the sake of a second child, we were a one-mother-one-daughter kind of race.

In an attempt to pull my foot out of my mouth, I pivoted verbally to the subject I'd lured Oyo into my room to talk about. "What I should have said is—your solution to Kira's problem was both thoughtful and clever. And, speaking of clever, I was curious how you knew Kira and I were living here with the Atwood pack?"

After all, werewolves and kitsunes weren't a predictable combination. And the two of us had been in wolf territory for only a few minutes before Oyo showed up.

"I'm not that clever," Oyo evaded, turning her back to slip out of her robe and into the borrowed clothing. "You're clever to convince werewolves to protect you. It's something I've never seen before."

"They'll protect you too." Her shoulders looked so slender, all hunched over with cold or fear as she faced away from me. But I squashed my immediate impulse to accept the change of subject and returned to my original point instead. "We'll all protect you. But it'll be easier if we know who might be following and what kind of trail you left behind. Did..."

Only I received no answer. Because Oyo was shifting, the air around her shimmering as she shrunk down into fox form right inside her borrowed clothing.

Then Allen's voice came through the closed door behind her—"Everybody decent? If so, the boss brought breakfast. Better get out here before Kira puts it all inside her hollow leg."

Whether or not Allen's approach had been what originally spooked her, Oyo was thoroughly terrified now. She scurried for cover under my bed, wisp of a fox tail tucking away into the darkness behind her. Then—if my ears served me right—she started clawing through drywall in search of an even safer hiding place.

So I wasn't getting any answers to my questions this morning. Well, I'd do my best to be patient. "Lead on," I told the waiting werewolf as I opened the door and greeted Allen with an almost-genuine smile on my face.

"LOOK, MAI, GOBS OF bacon!"

Someone must have fed my sister sugar, because she was bouncing off the walls...almost literally. Behind her, Gunner raised his eyebrows at me by way of greeting, and I couldn't quite tell if he'd been out righting wrongs or just hunting down food for the hyperactive teenager in our midst.

"I need to talk to you," Gunner mouthed, his expression not as welcoming as I would have hoped for. But Kira was hanging onto my shoulders now, trying to leap up so I'd carry her piggyback.

"Kira, you're strangling me!"

"Am not," my sister countered, but she did slide off long enough to stuff an entire piece of French toast into her mouth. Which, in turn, gave me the opportunity to slip past her without being drawn deeper into her sugar rush.

"I'm on Kira duty this morning," Allen promised as I walked toward his alpha. Then I was up close and personal with Gunner, whose face was still surprisingly grim. His fingers on my arm, however, were gentle as he guided me through the living room and out the front door.

"You know I want you and Kira here," he started without a formal greeting. And as much as I'd been looking forward to spending a moment alone together, I suddenly wished I could join Oyo in her hole in my bedroom wall.

Still, it was always better to rip off the proverbial bandaid quickly. So, sure Gunner was going no place I wanted to follow, I still prodded him to continue. "But?"

"No 'but.'" Gunner hesitated, then lowered himself down onto the top porch step, placing his head a good distance below mine. This wasn't the behavior of an alpha werewolf about to evict someone from his territory. And even though I appreciated his gesture, I still found myself sinking down right alongside him so I wouldn't end up towering above his head.

"Gunner, you're scaring me."

"There's no need to be scared." His huge hand landed on mine, furless and clawless and perfectly human. Still, I could *feel* the wolf vibrating inside him, itching to get out and hold this conversation in the two-legger's place. Given the fact that my fox form was a fraction the size of his animal, that realization wasn't a heartening feeling at all.

"I have a single request," he continued, unaware of my continued trepidation. "And you are free to ignore it if you feel it restricts your range of movement unduly..."

"Gunner." Now I finally smiled, understanding at last what he was so on edge about. He wasn't getting ready to evict me to ease the strain on his pack mates. Instead, he was trying not to send me fleeing with wolf demands couched as human requests.

Given my past problems with similar behavior, the alpha's caution was sweet...but we were well beyond that stage. "Talk," I told him. "I'm not leaving unless you kick me out."

"And I'm not kicking you out." At least *that* got his lips moving. "Everything you did last night was powerful," Gunner continued, diving into the heart of the matter at last. "The pack bonds actually look better this morning than they did yesterday. Still not good, but you solved as much in one evening as I have in four months."

It made me feel good to hear that. And yet...Gunner had looked undeniably sour when I stepped into the kitchen this morning. "What's your request?" I prodded him.

"Next time you walk into danger, please take me with you," he growled. He pulled out a brand new cell phone, texted me its number right there and then. And yet, despite the humanity of the gesture, I could see his inner wolf wild and angry behind sienna human eyes.

The two-legged pack leader was impressed by my lancing of the pack's metaphorical boils. But his four-legged counterpart was terrified I could have been even more badly hurt. And he was right to have sat us down for this conversation, because for one split second I was spitting mad.

How *dared* he distrust my ability to protect myself from danger? How *dared* he make a fox come begging for a wolf's help every time she felt like taking a piss?

The anger washed over me...and out of me. Then I was taking Gunner's hand in mine, glad to see my fingers were no more furry than his had been.

Because I wouldn't have asked any less of Gunner. I wouldn't have wanted him running off into battle on his lonesome. So—

"I promise," I told him. "I won't do anything dangerous without telling you. As long as you make the same promise in return."

Chapter 13

We sealed the deal with a kiss...or would have if a shiny steel blade hadn't sliced down between us just as our lips were a whisper away from meeting.

"Really?" the voice emerged from the other end of the blade even as the weapon twisted so it menaced only me. "You want us to be trained by someone who doesn't notice an armed swordswoman walking up beside her in a public space?"

I tried to see who was speaking, but I couldn't move without slicing my own jugular. So I used half of my attention to create a metal choker around my sensitive neck while responding to the opponent I still couldn't see.

"You want to be trained? It seems like you already know what you're doing." With my words as cover, I materialized the other half of my magic into a sword that clanked ever so slightly as it settled on the step below me.

Meanwhile, Gunner—darn him—merely chuckled as he stood and descended down the stairs away from the female with her sword at my neck. "Looks like you're busy," he noted. "How about we meet up for lunch later?"

"What happened to our promise?" I complained. "You watch my back, I watch your back?"

"You appear to have everything under control."

As we bantered, I used half my senses to guess how many werewolves had snuck up on us. Because I wasn't just facing the single female whose blade was now separated from me by a thin sheet of magical metal. No, from the scents and sounds, I'd guess there were half a dozen here at least.

Despite his dismissal, Gunner still hovered, ready to assist me. But this was clearly a problem I needed to solve myself. The trick was to make my escape not only effective but also flashy enough to prevent a repeat occurrence....

Stepping onto my sword hilt with one foot, I flicked it upward with the other. Then I twirled and caught my own weapon even as I used the metallic choker to knock my opponent's blade aside.

Edward's daughter. I wasn't sure whether to be pleased or daunted by the fact that my opponent was instantly recognizable. Ditto by the sheer number of females arrayed behind her back.

There were fifteen bystanders, most young but a few middle-aged or older. Becky wasn't among them, and even though a few faces looked vaguely familiar I didn't know anybody's name. Had they really come to me for lessons, or was this the female version of the welcoming committee that had left me black and blue yesterday when I failed to respect my place within the pack?

Whatever the sword wielder's purpose, I didn't slow my steps to debrief her nor did I bother to introduce myself. Instead, I slipped beneath my primary opponent's guard, gauging my angle carefully. She was clearly a clothes hog, her outfit perfectly coordinated and apparently tailored to her form.

So I hit her where it hurt the most. Turning my blade at an angle, I sliced off the lace collar lining the top half of her shirt. Her free hand rose to catch the descending fabric even as I slashed slices into her tight-fitting pants.

There was an art to ruining clothes without scratching the skin beneath it. Good thing I was a pro at that art.

Behind her, the other werewolves were wide-eyed, some gasping, a few giggling. Meanwhile, Edward's daughter seemed torn between anger...and was that amusement fighting for dominance on her face?

I'd almost forgotten Gunner was waiting until he spoke into the silence. "Yep, you definitely have this covered," Gunner noted. "Enjoy your girl time." And he strode away down the sidewalk, leaving me to teach swordsmanship to females who might or might not actually want to be taught.

"I'M ELIZABETH," EDWARD'S daughter told me as she shifted her sword to her left hand and stretched out the other so we could shake on it. "And you're impressive."

"Well, you're clearly not a beginner yourself," I countered, providing a bit of well-deserved praise to reduce the sting of her recent loss.

"Gunner gave us a DVD to practice with in August," the youngest girl interjected from behind the group's spokeswoman. "But it's hard to understand if you're not face to face with your teacher."

"So we'll practice face to face," I assured her. "Just give me a minute to gather some gear...." And I headed back up to the cottage in search of face masks and blade protectors, glad

I'd packed all of my teaching equipment even though Gunner hadn't bothered to give me a heads-up about my soon-to-be place within his clan prior to my move.

I had this covered, though. So it was hard to blame Gunner for his omission as we started with the basics, giving me time to take stock of my students one by one. They were better than I would have expected after just two months of DVD lessons, but they *did* have shifter agility to call upon after all.

Still, there were inevitable blunders. "No, not like that," I corrected, stepping up to place my own hand over the hilt of the oldest woman's weapon. "You want to—"

"—Get back in the kitchen where you belong!"

We all turned to face the interrupter of our lesson, and I didn't need to see the pack bonds or smell the sulfur to know there was definite rot developing between this twenty-something bystander and the females armed with swords. What I couldn't decipher was the reason for the former's venom. Had he been spurned by one of the young ladies, or was he simply threatened by any shift to the status quo?

"If you'd like to join us," I told the male carefully while waving in the appropriate direction, "there are extra masks over on the porch."

"*Join* you?" The werewolf looked like he'd smelled something vile. And maybe he had with his head stuffed so high up his own butt. "I'd rather f—"

"*Move it.*"

Yet again, a werewolf had snuck up on me while I wasn't looking. But this time the arriving shifter was a friend. Tank's hand landed on the other male's shoulder so hard the latter stumbled and almost fell to the pavement. Nonetheless, the nameless male puffed up his chest and opened his mouth to spew out more invective...until, that is, his gaze and Tank's met.

I reached out my hand, wanting to warn Tank that fighting my battles wasn't going to help matters in the long run. But Gunner's lieutenant was too intent upon subduing his opponent with a single glance. Sure enough, our unwelcome audience member shriveled beneath Tank's stare-down, turning without another word and beating it out of sight.

"I guess that's our cue to get back to work," I noted, trying to keep frustration out of my voice. How was I supposed to do my job as the alpha's mate if well-meaning werewolves kept stepping in and doing that work for me?

But this time Tank's gaze met mine as he shook his head. "They'll have to finish up by themselves, chica. Because there's someone here to see you. She says she's your grandmother."

Chapter 14

randmother. It was almost as if my struggles with Kira and the resultant yearnings had created a family member where none previously existed. Not even realizing I was leaving Tank behind me, I padded down the road in the direction he must have come from, drawn forward by what I suspected was a pack-like bond but couldn't confirm without werewolf blood to energize my latent skills.

Only, it turned out I didn't need a turbocharge to solve the mystery. Because an old woman with a fox-like cant to her neck walked spryly out to meet me. "Granddaughter." She was tiny but not wizened. Clearly Japanese in a way my sister and I were not. The stranger-who-wasn't-a-stranger inclined her head ever so slightly, then frowned when I fumbled through a mirroring nod by way of reply.

And that show of disapproval was enough to knock loose my rose-tinted glasses. Family connection or no, it was time to remember that I was in charge of my own destiny. Step one: Figure out how and why kitsunes—because this was clearly another kitsune—kept showing up on our doorstep. Step two: Get rid of this particular kitsune before the pack blew its collective lid.

So, ignoring the fact that I was sorely in need of an older family member who had a clue how to raise a teenager, I forced my voice to turn hard as I demanded: "How did you find us?"

But the old woman was having none of it. "I'll answer all of your questions, granddaughter," she told me, "but not standing out here in the cold. Remember—patience is bitter..."

"...But its fruit is sweet." Despite myself, I mouthed the end of the proverb right alongside her, remembering the way Mama had admonished me with those exact same words when I child-ishly complained about inevitable daily delays.

And maybe that's why I didn't protest when this elderly stranger led me back down the street away from my cottage and toward an RV parked at the edge of the Green where break-fast had been served yesterday evening. Maybe that's why I didn't pull out my sword and threaten five of the most hand-some males I'd ever seen—the old woman's entourage?—as they brushed past me to begin cranking out the vehicle's walls.

Even without benefit of the additions, the RV was the largest one I'd ever seen. "Wow." I didn't mean to, but the word emerged from my mouth as easily as if I was Kira and always spoke before I thought.

"One of many benefits of our heritage, granddaughter," the old woman told me, face mischievous as if she was letting me in on the first secret of many she'd been saving just for me. But rather than elaborating, she raised both eyebrows, slipped up the stairs someone had set out for her, then disappeared inside.

I itched to follow, but I didn't immediately. Instead, I turned and peered back toward the spot we'd recently left be-hind.

I'd only been gone for a moment, but already the female werewolves had dispersed, taking Tank along with them. Instead, Gunner had reappeared, broad shoulders sagging ever so slightly from the weight of his load. Meanwhile, the air between us smelled just a little bit foul with the same scent that hung around clan central every time something was gearing up to go wrong.

I was adding to that load—and perhaps to that scent?—by spending time with this supposed grandmother. And yet...I couldn't quite talk myself into telling this strange kitsune to leave without discovering whether she really was related to me first.

So, without meeting Gunner's eyes or requesting his permission, I clambered up the stairs and entered the unknown.

"YOU MAY CALL ME SOBO," the old woman informed me as I stepped into a space perfectly designed to fit everything one woman and five men might need in their living room. There were two couches, a recliner, heat blowing out of wall registers, a picture window opening onto forest, and even a large TV covering the opposite wall.

Despite the various seating areas, however, two of her companions—definitely human if my nose served me—knelt on either side of Sobo's easy chair. Both gazed up at her adoringly, and in response she patted their heads as if they were dogs.

That was...odd. But I was here for answers, not to pass judgment. So I walked deeper into the old woman's domain, feeling the door click shut behind me, presumably closed by yet another member of Sobo's silent entourage.

And that's enough of thinking about random humans, I reminded myself. Ignoring the males' strange behavior, I instead rolled the unfamiliar name around in my mouth like a new food I wasn't quite sure I liked the flavor of. "Sobo," I repeated aloud.

"My name is Sakurako," the old woman clarified. "But it is appropriate that my granddaughter call me Sobo instead. It means grandmother. Or, maybe...grandma?"

And even though I hated myself for being so simple, the idea that I was being offered a pet name melted the cold ache that had settled in my stomach ever since Kira started treating me like an enemy rather than a friend. It reminded me of the days when I hadn't been the matriarch of my own tiny family, when Mama had called me Mai-chan and hugged me close up against her waist before spinning me around the kitchen in our own made-up dance.

Blinking away that seductive memory, I forced myself to remember Oyo's fear and the problems facing Atwood clan central. Even if Sobo was my relative, that wasn't the most important point to consider now.

So I remained standing rather than taking a seat on the couch Sobo motioned to. And I repeated my own words from earlier, this time demanding a reply. "How did you find us?" I asked a second time, piercing the old woman with a gaze that refused to be sidetracked by proverbs, a luxurious residence, or even familial love.

"Direct, just like your mother." For the first time since I'd met her, Sobo seemed uncomfortable, shifting on the plush leather beneath her. And just like Mama when she was unhappy, Sobo's face remained smooth save her cheek, which twitched ever so slightly up by her left eye.

I opened my mouth, struck by the similarity. Before I could relent, however, Sobo answered my question.

"I felt the moment your sister merged with her star ball," Sobo told me. "I thought that was *your* coming of age, actually. What a...surprise...to discover my daughter chose undue fertility over long life."

I knew this wasn't the whole story. It wasn't lost upon me that—if her story was to be believed—our grandmother had felt Kira's presence four months earlier and in an entirely different spot from the one where she'd finally tracked us down.

Still, the tremor in the old woman's hands told the truth of her pain at the loss of a daughter. The sad bend of Sobo's neck was so much like Mama's during her darkest hours that I sank down onto the couch despite myself and cupped her papery fingers in both of my hands.

Whether or not this old woman was here under false pretenses, I believed she was my grandmother. And that meant she deserved my compassion and respect.

"Sobo, I'm sorry," I murmured. And I could feel the bonds of family clicking closed between us with my touch.

Chapter 15

"That must have come as a shock," I continued, trying to send warm healing energy into the older woman through both my words and my fingers. The two humans flanking us leaned in closer, like dogs offering comfort through their presence alone.

"It was a disappointment," the older woman countered. But rather than pulling away from my touch, she squeezed my fingers one second longer while offering me the fairy tale I'd spent a decade pretending I didn't crave with the yearning of an orphaned fox pup.

"*You*, however, were not a disappointment," my grandmother informed me. "I have long searched for a granddaughter. A firm, strong woman to train and to nurture. A brave kitsune to carry on the family name after I leave this plane."

As she spoke, she gazed at me with eyes so dark they might as well have been Mama's. There was a warmth to her smile now, a pride that seemed to stroke my cheeks while making my spine straighten.

And like a fish in a pond, I rose toward the bobber, opened my mouth to accept the offered nourishment. Of course, bait inevitably comes with a fish hook. But at that moment, I didn't even care that this was bound to end in pain....

Before I could speak, however, Sakurako continued, "I just need one small favor from you, granddaughter. Nothing major. No skin off your teeth."

"Yes, Sobo?" I nudged her when she turned silent.

Rather than answering, the old woman peered at me for one long moment, her pursed lips reminding me so much of Mama's that my breath caught in my throat. Then, finally, she told me the price of becoming part of her family.

"All I need from you," she finished, "is that black fox you and your sister are hiding. Oyo is difficult, dangerous. Too much for you to handle on your own without further training. Turn her over to me to take care of, then we can build up our family as it should be with the next generation at its heart."

"OF COURSE, SOBO."

I could feel the words lingering there on the tip of my tongue, ready to escape if I unclenched my teeth and let my mouth fall open. Which was absurd given that what Sakurako was asking was both dishonorable and patently unwise...while also going against my oath to the black-furred kitsune both Gunner and I had promised to protect.

Worse was the knowledge that the woman before me wasn't manipulating me via magic the way Liam had done four months earlier. No, this decision—chosen family versus blood family—would be mine to make and mine alone.

I couldn't say no and I wouldn't say yes, so I merely disentangled my hand from Sakurako's and stepped backwards. Meanwhile, the old woman's words flew after me like a thrusting sword.

"Next time I see you, granddaughter, I will expect your answer."

And I couldn't even shake my head as I stumbled out the door and shut it between us. My answer. I had no answer. Wouldn't bring even more conflict to this ailing pack, and at the same time couldn't talk myself into giving either Sakurako or Oyo away.

I have a grandmother. A manipulative grandmother who appeared to possess a heart of ice, but a grandmother nonetheless.

Striding blindly down the street, I imagined for one awestruck moment becoming part of a large, loving family. Possessing older, wiser family members able and willing to steer me away from bad decisions before the results slapped me in the face.

Why did even dreaming of such a rosy picture feel like a mistake?

I was so lost in the confusion of my roiling feelings that I nearly walked past the two werewolves half-hidden by the trunk of the oak tree that spread huge and magnificent across the pack's gathering space. But I couldn't miss the sulfurous stench that rose around me, cuing me to extend my senses just as Gunner murmured, "I understand that Edward."

"*You* understand? I don't think you do, *alpha*," Edward countered. And, through the brush, I could just barely see him shake off Gunner's physical show of support so violently that any other pack leader would have taken mortal offense at the slight. As it was, I could barely smell the faintest hint of electricity invading the sulfur as Gunner tamped his frustration down enough to reply.

"I understand you thought this pack was worth saving or you wouldn't have stayed when so many others left with my brother," Gunner answered, not a single growl in his tone even though his voice grew firmer as his statement progressed. "I ask that you remember our purpose here before..."

"Before you act like a spiteful child and tear up everything your father built? Before your kitsune concubine makes so many mistakes there's no pack to even attempt saving? You let her do this even though she's not really your mate?"

Edward was so red-faced, I was a little afraid he might succumb to a heart attack. A little afraid...and also very faintly hoping that the greatest rabble-rouser in Atwood territory would take himself out of the picture without either me or Gunner having to do the deed ourselves. *Concubine, my ass.*

"Edward." Now Gunner did finally growl out a chastisement.

"Don't bark at me, Gunner." Edward stood taller as he spoke, a sure sign of a werewolf in search of a fur-form turf battle. "I remember when you were a toddler gnawing on your father's fingers. I never thought I'd see the day you forgot your duty over some fox in a skirt."

The last time I'd worn a skirt was during an ill-fated job interview. But I think we all got Edward's point, because this time Gunner's order was both more specific and more adamant. *"You will respect my mate."*

"I'll respect those who deserve respect," Edward countered. "And if you don't wake up and do your duty to this pack before kitsunes invite in our neighbors, then I'll correct my own mistake and join your brother in exile. You know half the pack will follow me." He paused, then threw down the gauntlet. "And is it truly exile when no one but the weak are left behind?"

I only realized my fists were clenched and my sword visible when the tip of the latter caught in the hem of my trousers and nearly tripped me. *Okay, that's not helping matters*, I chided, imagining literally stumbling into Gunner and Edward's conversation before falling flat on my face.

Edward would be enraged. Gunner would be mortified. No, that definitely wouldn't help defuse the older male's anger...but what would?

My fingers slid across the face of my cell phone, Ransom's unanswered text rising up in my mind's eye. *"I grant you free passage to and from Kelleys Island if you'd like to come and talk about it."*

The message suddenly seemed less like a trap and more like much-needed breathing space given the drama I'd be leaving behind.

Chapter 16

Relieved of her load of boxes, Old Red rumbled down the highway with fewer complaints than she'd regaled me with previously. Unfortunately, that didn't make me feel any better about driving away from Atwood pack central at the exact moment when my sister and Oyo needed me most.

Beep!

Glancing sideways at the empty passenger seat, I couldn't help smiling at Kira's text. *"Stop worrying. I'm fine,"* she chided. Clearly, Oyo's pep talk—and the chocolate, potato chips, and hot-water bottle I'd left the teenager with—had rebooted her ailing mood.

I would have replied, too, but Old Red was far from a driverless vehicle. In fact, she was prone to drifting sideways, a problem that I knew would be remedied once I got the tires balanced and aligned.

But I'd stopped accepting Gunner's financial support the moment Kira was adopted, and my part-time summer gig teaching fencing at the Y hadn't paid very well. A wolf wouldn't have batted an eyelash at accepting pack largesse, but I was very much a fox shifter. So while my bank account slowly grew into an appreciable buffer, I kept my hands very firmly grasping the wheel.

A difficult matter when the chime of another incoming text drew my eyes to the phone a second time in a matter of moments. *"Nobody's eaten me or Oyo. Not even when we played fox tag on Allen and Tank's heads. That was really fun."*

Flicking on the turn signal in the direction of the ferry dock, Oyo's black fur dueled with the sienna tinge of Gunner's irises in my mind's eye. The pack seemed to be doing quite well without me present. So why did I feel so guilty about taking a fox-like stab at the heart of the problem on my own?

Guilty or guiltless, I was almost there and the decision was long since made. Old Red's brakes squealed as I pulled to a halt behind two other cars lined up at the ticket booth. And I took advantage of the lack of forward momentum to text Kira back. *"Remember you're a guest in Atwood clan central,"* I told her. *"Take care of Oyo but be smart about it."*

Then I turned away from the phone and tuned up my senses. Because I wasn't safely secluded in Atwood territory with Oyo and my sister. Instead, I'd spent the last few hours passing through outpack land where lawless werewolves did as they pleased...which likely included slaughtering vagrant kitsunes on sight.

As if my thoughts had called danger into existence, hairs rose along the back of my neck half a second before a knock shook the nearest window. Inhaling sharply, I turned to take in the visage of a werewolf...and not one I was familiar with either.

This male was just as tall and broad as Gunner. But his face was craggier, as if he'd been punched a dozen times then healed without courtesy of a doctor visit. Not a pack wolf then.

The question became—was my window rapper a curious stranger, or the outguard watching over Ransom's exiled lair?

"GET OUT."

His voice was soft, barely a whisper. But it carried through the window and stroked tendrils of ice up and down my spine. And while my impulse was to make a U-turn and head back up the highway, I instead rolled down the window a fraction of an inch, raised my chin, and sniffed.

Because I should have been able to tell if this male was Ransom's lackey by the presence or absence of that tongue-tingling ozone. And I also could have, perhaps, detected his loyalty by the presence or absence of a rotten-egg smell.

Unfortunately, all I could make out from inside my metal cocoon was the overwhelming stench of diesel, tar, and half-rotten fish emanating from the nearby lake.

"Why should I?" I asked, playing for time while I calculated other options. One car had already rolled past the ticket booth while the driver in the second vehicle was busy buying a pass for the ferry loading at the end of the road. If I waited until the coast was clear, perhaps I could gun it and apologize to the humans for not paying even as I left this werewolf behind on the mainland....

"Not gonna happen," the male said, clearly picking up on my plans via scent and body language. "Get out," he repeated. "Ransom wants me to take you across in our boat."

Get on a boat with an unknown werewolf? Even if this stranger knew I was here to meet Ransom, the answer was still nopety, nope, nope, nope.

The wind changed at that moment, pushing the werewolf's scent through the crack and into my nostrils. He smelled of wet gravel and newly mown lawn without a hint of ozone...which, unfortunately, could have meant anything at all. I didn't know enough about werewolves to understand whether their scents shifted when they evicted themselves from a pack as a unit. So I didn't really know if a loyal ally of Gunner's brother would still boast the distinctive Atwood scent.

"I'd prefer to stick to the original plan," I countered just as my phone trilled from the passenger seat. And even though, instinct demanded that I keep my attention tuned to the stranger, I still couldn't resist glancing down at the screen.

"Eric is mine," Ransom had texted, making me shiver and peer out across the nearly empty parking area to figure out how the alpha had known I was balking at the pickup. There was nothing to see, however. Just the ticket booth, the waiting ferry, and a couple of empty vehicles parked off to one side.

Which meant Ransom was guessing, playing cat and mouse with me. Too bad for him that I was a fox instead of a mouse.

A fox who noted what Ransom *hadn't* said as much as what he *had* said. The exiled alpha had been the one to invite me into his not-quite-territory in the first place, and he hadn't issued an ultimatum telling me to ride across with Eric or go home without the offered meeting either.

Which meant Ransom wanted this get-together as much as I did. Had as good as handed over leverage to use against this shifter guarding the virtual gate.

While I pondered, the unnamed werewolf had been padding around the vehicle like a stalking panther. And the fact that he wasn't hovering directly over me made it just a little easier to expose my neck as I leaned over to pop open the lock on the passenger-side door.

"I'm not getting on a boat alone with a strange werewolf," I said once I'd straightened. "But if you want to ride across with me on the public ferry, then I'm game."

Chapter 17

Thirty minutes cooped up in Old Red alongside a simmering werewolf felt like three hours. But it was better than the alternative—jumping out of the parked vehicle and letting Eric wander around behind my back.

So I stuck it out, made the bare minimum pleasantries, and allowed the shifter to guide me to my destination after the ferry workers finally ushered us off the floating prison on the other side. "Left," Eric grunted as we turned onto the main street, rolling past huge houses with green, sweeping lawns and lakeside vistas. Ransom might have left Atwood pack central with nothing more than the clothes on his back, but he appeared to have landed quite solidly on his feet.

"Here," Eric said at last, as we passed an ice-cream parlor crowded with hungry tourists then a small but well-maintained city park. My guide barely waited for the car to slow before opening his door and hurrying down the sidewalk away from me. By the time I'd pulled the key from the ignition, he was already out of sight.

"Now what?" I murmured, sniffing the air surreptitiously. It would be hard to find Eric's scent in the midst of all of these tourists, people pressing past me as I blocked the flow of the human tide....

But I needn't have worried. Because as I turned in a slow circle, I caught sight of Ransom watching from behind a restaurant's plate-glass window. The elder Atwood brother was cupping a mug of coffee, his shoulders hunched ever so subtly. As if being a pack leader in exile was harder than he'd initially assumed.

Or maybe that was just my imagination. Because as our gazes snapped together, my breath caught in reaction. *This* wasn't the look of a beaten-down pack leader; it was the stare of a two-legged predator trying to decide whether I'd be better eaten with biscuits or toast.

Run, run, run, instinct told me. And I had to forcibly pry my fingers away from the car door to prevent myself from hopping back inside and gunning it out of there.

We were separated by thirty feet of air and a thick pane of glass, so Ransom couldn't smell my terror. Still, he must have noted the change in my demeanor anyway. Because his mouth spread into his characteristic smirking smile. Then, crooking a single finger, he raised his eyebrows and motioned for me to approach.

"SICK OF MY BROTHER already?" the elder Atwood sibling greeted me as the door whooshed shut behind my back. My muscles tensed in reaction, the reality of being stuck inside a nearly empty restaurant with an alpha werewolf who smelled of fur giving me the urge to turn on my heel and hurry back the way I'd come.

I was done retreating however. Instead, it was time to attack.

"This isn't about your brother," I countered as I padded forward on the balls of my feet, magic whirling invisibly around my fingers. "This is about loose lips and strangers suddenly knowing that clan Atwood has taken in two kitsunes. How did that information go mainstream, do you think?"

"Perhaps you should ask my brother," Ransom countered, bringing the conversation back where he clearly wanted it to stay. "But—wait—Gunner doesn't know you came to speak with me or you'd never be here unguarded. So what does that make *you* for sneaking out behind your alpha's back?"

A mate rather than a sycophant, I wanted to answer, never mind Edward's assessment of the matter. But, instead, I merely shrugged and murmured, "A fox."

Despite my best intentions to hold myself wolf-like and tall, I couldn't prevent my body from swiveling as I spoke, cringing at having my identity outed in a public space. Because I wasn't on Atwood turf any longer where pack-leader compulsion required that kitsunes be treated respectfully. Good thing the restaurant really was as empty as I'd initially supposed.

Ransom's laugh brought my head back around to face him. "A cagey fox," he agreed, pouring a packet of sugar into his coffee then stirring the liquid around with a plastic straw. "But you want something, now don't you? Which means you'll give me something in return."

Ah, here we go. Slipping into the booth across from him, I leaned forward despite the instinct that told me not to squeeze myself into an enclosed space with an alpha wolf. "Perhaps," I answered. And since werewolves were big fans of dominance rituals, I met and held his gaze for several long seconds after that.

Ransom had eyes exactly like his brother's. Deep and brown and not quite dark enough to appear black even in dimly lit corners. Also like his brother, Ransom smelled of Atwood ozone, the scent so sharp it made the hairs inside my nostrils itch.

Unlike Gunner, however, Ransom was always on the hunt for an overt show of submission. "I want your debt," he told me now, voice smooth as silk caressed by sunlight. "Like the debt you owed my brother, to be called in whenever I wish."

I shook my head, not so much in rejection as in denial of the situation. Because what Ransom apparently failed to realize was that, by coming to him for a favor, I'd already accepted that I'd owe a brand new debt to this exiled werewolf. Accepted that...along with the wedge I knew it would form between myself and his brother, the same brother who called himself my mate.

"No?" Ransom prodded.

"You're an idiot," I answered, my words unheated. "Yes, I will be in your debt to the degree you help me track down this kitsune's history."

As I spoke, I pulled out my cell phone, Oyo's picture already drawn up on its screen. I didn't have any image of my grandmother, but Kira had snapped this shot after our bonding ritual then had texted the image to me for use in my questioning.

I didn't explain any of that to Ransom, however. Instead, I angled the phone in his direction while bracing myself for smug recognition. After all, the feelers Gunner had put out this morning suggested the neighboring packs were, indeed, sending an unusual number of messages back and forth between the clans. Which pointed a finger at the brother who had means, motive, and opportunity to throw the original Atwood pack to the neighboring wolves.

But all I got from Ransom was cold intensity. "Name?" he demanded as he stared at my phone's screen.

"Oyo," I answered. I hadn't thought to request a surname while she was human so I had nothing else to provide other than a reiteration of my original request. "Do you have any idea who might know that foxes now live within Gunner's pack?"

"No," the exiled alpha answered, head shaking as his resemblance to Gunner deepened. Then, giving me the answer I wanted but for a reason I couldn't quite decipher: "But I certainly intend to find out."

Chapter 18

Despite my relatively benign conversation with Ransom, I was no more confident that werewolves would leave me alone when I emerged from the restaurant than I had been going into it. Sure enough, the air when I stepped out onto the sidewalk was redolent with fur, and I found my feet moving faster than I'd intended as I scurried back toward my car.

Inside, I flicked the locks, turned the key in the ignition...then noticed that the engine-temperature gauge wasn't as cold as I'd expected after a prolonged resting period. Biting my lip, I considered popping the hood and checking coolant levels. But I couldn't afford for Ransom to see inside the trunk if I went rooting around for the requisite tools....

Meanwhile, during those few seconds I pondered car repair, a mob of werewolves had already materialized, traveling rapidly toward me from opposite ends of the street. Sandwiched in the middle were dozens of human tourists, bound to spook at a shifter altercation that could attract the attention of non-shifter police.

So I'll deal with potential overheating on the ferry, I decided. After all, that shifter-free zone was only a few minutes' drive away.

Backing out of my parking spot, a werewolf snarled from inches behind my taillights. Slamming down my foot to pull forward away from him, I almost ran over the one familiar shifter standing two-legged in front of my car.

Elle. She was brown-eyed just like Gunner and Ransom, and now that I knew her heritage I could easily see the resemblance to both brothers in her face.

In human parlance, Elle was my sister-in-law. She was also my mentor and one of the most friendly werewolves I'd ever met. During stolen afternoons spread across the previous summer, we'd talked about everything from kitsune magic to girly gossip. And, in the process, we must have started building a pack bond because I now felt my body lean toward her as something immaterial tugged at my gut.

"Meet me at the ferry dock. I'll buy you a coffee," the other female mouthed, the words easy to pick out despite the smeared glass of my windshield. In that moment, it was hard to remember that we hadn't written or spoken since Elle and her mate left with Ransom rather than staying in Atwood clan central with the rest of us.

Our incipient friendship had been frozen by the stubbornness of two pack leaders, Gunner mandating that no exile could return even for a visit and Ransom retaliating with the order that no communication was allowed between the two clans at all. So Elle and I had lost the chance to talk, not only about shared interests but also about the fact that I was the one responsible for her twin brother's death.

I'd never been able to make that loss up to her, but Elle must have found it in her heart to forgive me anyway. Because her eyes now crinkled up into a smile, and I felt my own face opening happily in response.

This moment was our chance to thaw our relationship. To place it in the sun, water it, and watch it grow.

And yet...I couldn't do that. Not when Elle and I had made our respective decisions about pack affiliation months earlier. Not when I risked so much by parking Old Red on Kelleys Island a minute longer than I absolutely had to.

So shaking my head then averting my eyes from Elle's crestfallen expression, I drove away from her down the street.

I MADE IT APPROXIMATELY a quarter of the way back to clan central before a white cloud started gushing out from beneath the hood of my vehicle. *Oops.* I'd let the disappointment on Elle's face sidetrack me, and now Old Red was paying the price.

"Shh, quiet, you can do this," I crooned at my ancient sedan as I pulled her over to the side of the highway. Was that steam or smoke emerging through cracks in the metal? It suddenly looked more like the latter, with gray twisting up to spiral through the white.

"No! You can't do this!" I demanded, forcing myself not to pound on the steering wheel. "You know why you can't do this...." Even alone in the vehicle in outpack territory, I couldn't quite make myself mention the precious cargo still stashed in the trunk.

I *could* do something about the upcoming disaster however. Ignoring the wind of a passing tractor-trailer shaking the vehicle around me, I frantically pulled levers at my feet before thrusting open the door. A car honked in protest, swerving away but still coming far too close for comfort. Meanwhile, my attention flew straight to the gas tank and I swore loudly—I'd opened the wrong metal lid by mistake.

Hopping back into the driver's seat, I looked down this time as I hunted for plastic handles beside my feet. *There.* I wasn't quite breathing as I located the appropriate lever then emerged a second time.

Emerged into smoke that choked me even as I raced away from the front end of the vehicle. Had noxious gases gathered in the rear compartment that wasn't intended to carry passengers? Had...?

"Breathe." Gunner emerged from the trunk, his arms settled around me even as he drew me away from Old Red at a trot. Together, we fled as fleetly as two-legged shifters are able to. And despite the fact that he had spent hours hiding in the trunk to provide backup without spooking his brother, I was the one shaking as we raced backwards away from my car.

Gunner is fine, I reminded myself. *Get it together.* And, finally, the alpha's solid presence beside me was enough to provide breathing room in which to glance back over my shoulder at the smoking car we'd so recently left behind.

"It's not going to explode," my mate promised. Then, rightly understanding my body's twitch, he corrected himself. "*She.* She's not going to explode. But Old Red might not be quite the same after this."

And that was okay as long as Gunner was safely beside me rather than asphyxiating in the trunk of the still smoking vehicle. I squeezed his hand hard enough to be certain I wasn't dreaming...then I buried my face in his shoulder so I wouldn't have to watch the devastation of what had been my pride and joy the day before.

Old Red wasn't much, but she was my first stab at self-owned transportation. It was hard watching her erupt into a cloud of smoke.

"You probably want to know about Ransom," I murmured into the fabric of Gunner's sweatshirt, attempting to distract myself.

"I do. But first let me call a tow truck."

Which—capable werewolf—he managed to do without dislodging my limpet-like attachment to his body. The moment of letting him fix everything served as a balm to my soul.

Still, I wasn't used to being dependent on anyone else to solve my problems. So by the time Gunner hung up the phone, I was ready to take a peek at my car—no longer smoking quite so badly—then to answer the questions that had to be rolling through Gunner's head.

"He didn't know anything about Oyo, but he said he'd ask around for us." Then, taking a step backwards without separating our intertwined fingers, I relayed the part I would have been worried about in his place. "Your brother looked tired but healthy," I informed him. Ransom had also appeared predatory and wolfish. But the tiredness, I figured, was what Gunner most wanted to know about.

"Leading a pack is hard work," the alpha beside me rumbled, pulling me back up against his skin.

And now that I thought about it, Gunner boasted the same predatory stance his brother did, along with the same world-weary cant to his neck. So maybe Old Red imploding would lead to something good after all. Because Gunner sorely needed a break from his pack, craved a little time to forget how badly divided formerly close friends had become.

"What if we got a room and dealt with transportation in the morning?" I suggested before Gunner could place the call he'd queued up to his second-in-command. Sure, someone could come get us...but would it kill the pack for us to steal one evening for ourselves before that occurred?

I held my breath, expecting Gunner's responsibilities to take precedence over his own wishes. Only, this time I turned out to be mistaken.

"That's the best suggestion I've heard in hours," my mate rumbled. Then, preventing me from answering in the easiest way possible, he bent down to complete our far-too-often-interrupted kiss.

Chapter 19

U nfortunately, everything crumbled once we reached our rundown motel on the seedy side of town. The problem wasn't the accommodations, either. In fact, by the time we checked in, I had eyes for one thing only: the bed.

It was queen-sized, just right for two people who liked each other and hadn't been in the same zip code for an entire season. Plus, Gunner and I had shared a house with keen-eared shifters even when we cohabited, which added to my body's frustration by quite a lot.

So, toeing out of my shoes, I took his hand and tugged him in the appropriate direction before shedding layer after layer of clothing. "Mates shouldn't spend so much time away from each other," I murmured, reaching over to tug Gunner's head down so his lips were within reach.

But his neck didn't bend as predicted. Nor did his clothes magically fly in the opposite direction the way I willed them to. Instead, Gunner's hands landed on my shoulders...and, very gently, he pushed me away from him until I fell into a seated position on the edge of the bed.

"Gunner?" I started, then went quiet so I could hear what he was muttering.

"Allen was right, the bastard," he growled, his words clearly not intended for me.

Allen not Edward? I remembered Edward calling me a concubine—understandable given his antipathy toward fox shifters. But I'd thought Allen liked me. The geeky werewolf certainly seemed willing to come when I pulled on his pack bond.

I was about to request clarification when Gunner finally met my eyes and offered exactly what I was about to ask for. "We aren't mates," he said, his simple words hitting me like a bombshell. "Well, you're my mate, but I'm not yours."

THE DETONATION EXPLODED deep within my belly, and like any wounded fox I lashed out in an attempt at self-preservation. "What are you talking about? I moved in with you, didn't I? I let myself get beaten up by werewolves. What greater commitment do you need than that?"

"I didn't ask you to fight my battles."

I should have known better than to bring up the ill-fated bacon episode. Still, the growled dismissal in Gunner's voice rubbed me entirely the wrong way.

Because I felt like I gave and gave and gave to this werewolf. Now he was telling me my compromises weren't good enough?

Which might explain why months of smoothed-over slights bubbled to the surface with the force of a volcanic eruption. "You said you wanted me to be part of the pack," I started, "so how exactly does that make my battles yours to take over? And let's talk about you insisting I take you with me to talk to Ransom. As if I'm just a weak woman who couldn't be trusted to deal with your brother on my own."

I hadn't realized how angry I was until I started speaking. How hurt I felt by werewolf instincts that might have been intended as supportive but instead came across as an undermining of my own authority and free will.

Gunner's patience, apparently, had been similarly strained by dealing with my vulpine nature. Or so I gathered as he snapped out his reply.

"I don't trust you to watch out for yourself because you don't do it," he spat back. "Perhaps you didn't notice the fact you almost died on the highway this evening? I *told* you that rustbucket wasn't safe enough to drive down the block let alone across the state."

"So you want to make another decision for me, is that it? You want to take over yet another aspect of my life?"

I expected him to yell a rebuttal. Because, yes, I was yelling. Heat suffused my face while my hands shook with the urge to turn into fists.

Only, Gunner didn't speak. Instead, he stalked over to the closet. Silently, he pulled the spare blanket and pillow off a shelf before retreating to a padded chair as far as he could get from the waiting mattress.

For my part, I headed in the opposite direction, swishing my mouth out in the bathroom while wishing I had toothpaste to cover the foul flavor of my own mistakes. Because my words—while based on reality—had been intentionally hurtful. Yes, Gunner stepped on my toes from time to time and impinged upon my autonomy. But my arguments became small and petty when I realized his only return complaint was that I didn't take good enough care of my own skin.

Whether or not I was wrong, I wasn't about to apologize. Not when doing so would relinquish the last shred of independence I clutched so frantically to my chest. Instead, I slipped alone between scratchy sheets while straining my ears in hopes Gunner would be the one to relent first.

And he did speak even though he didn't apologize. Instead, he explained what Allen had guessed and what I hadn't previously known.

"I'm going to spell it out for you," Gunner growled, his voice tight with barely restrained anger. "If you want to be my mate, it's a simple matter, although breaking a mate bond isn't easy and it isn't fun. So, be sure before you do it. Then say you're mated and I'll become your mate."

That was it? I opened my mouth to release words that would have ended the battle between us by confirming that I loved the frustrating yet adorable alpha curled into a chair on the other side of the hotel room. I opened my mouth...then choked as something stilled my tongue.

No, not something—some*one*. Or make that several someones.

Because promising myself to Gunner meant promising I wouldn't take Kira and flee if living in the pack became too dangerous. Meanwhile, a bond as ironclad as Gunner was suggesting meant his own pack might suffer if they were unable to come to terms with a kitsune in their midst.

My breath caught as I realized I was caught on a ledge with yawning crevasses on both the right hand and the left hand, with only one small path leading to safety on the other side. I fully expected Gunner to push me toward that knife-edge trail, demanding a declaration I wasn't ready for. But instead, he let me off the hook.

"It's not a choice to be made hastily," he continued, his voice gravelly with repressed emotion. "Until you tell me to leave you, I'll still be here."

He *was* still there...and was just as heavy-handed about his urge to take over my life as ever. I hadn't missed the fact there was no promise to abide by my future decisions emanating from the opposite side of the room.

So I did what foxes do best—I slid out from under a difficult situation. Sighing, I closed my eyes and waited for sleep to descend. Tonight, I'd recover my equanimity. Tomorrow would be plenty soon enough to figure out the puzzle of becoming an alpha werewolf's mate.

Chapter 20

I woke to an Atwood male leaning over me...but not the one I'd gone to bed with. Instead, it was Ransom's eyes gleaming with approval as he took in my unclad state.

"My brother should learn to share," he murmured, lips twisting into a smirking smile. I didn't smell any actual arousal and had a feeling he was just being a jerk. But that didn't prevent me from closing my fingers around a sword that was abruptly under the bedclothes along with me, just in case.

Then I remembered what was missing from this picture. Where was Gunner and why wasn't he tearing out his brother's throat?

For half a second, I thought last night's argument had been more divisive than even I realized. Then the hotel-room door banged open and Gunner came in backwards, his hands full of a paper bag and a container of steaming coffee cups.

"I got you a..." he started. Then liquid splattered as he dropped my breakfast—or maybe, from the height of the sun outside the window, lunch—ruining the already stained carpet in front of the door.

Before Gunner could shift or roar or just strangle his brother, I leapt out of bed to prevent cold-blooded fratricide. But both brothers remained rooted where they'd been when they first saw each other, more expressions than I could identify flitting across nearly identical faces.

"So you didn't let her come alone after all," Ransom murmured after a moment, taking a single step toward his brother and giving me the space to slip into my clothes.

"She's my mate. I don't leave her," Gunner answered. "But I held true to the letter of our agreement. I didn't set foot on the soil of your land."

And in that moment, I learned what a werewolf bond looked like when it was shattered. Like two brothers who itched to hug each other but instead stood separated by far more than ten feet of musty air.

I shivered, realizing that the dull ache I felt from having to refuse Elle was nothing compared to Gunner and Ransom's agony. But they could still fix this. All it would take was the right gesture of reconciliation and I knew both brothers would embrace the other and put the previous four months firmly in the past.

So I held my breath and waited. Waited so long, in fact, that I not only started breathing again but inhaled the scent of donuts disintegrating in a pool of coffee on the floor. And when it became clear that neither brother was willing or able to speak about the real issue, I decided it was finally time to break the ice.

"You found something about Oyo?" I suggested, stepping into the no-man's-land of empty space between the brothers.

"What I found out is that everyone and their mother knows Atwood clan central is home to kitsunes," Ransom agreed, his eyes meeting mine with what actually looked like gratitude. "One of the outpack males we took in last month heard the story and apparently thought it was a good idea to spread it around outside our territory. He won't make that mistake again."

So Ransom's pack really was the source of the leak...and the problem was larger than either Gunner or I had supposed. I shivered, wondering if less friendly kitsunes—and werewolves—would be showing up at clan central by the time we got home.

But it wasn't cool to shoot the messenger. "You can ask for what I owe you," I reminded the older Atwood brother. "I'll be glad to fulfill my debt."

"Later. Maybe," Ransom answered. Then as abruptly as he'd appeared above me, he brushed past his brother and padded out the door.

"THE CAR IS TOAST."

An hour later, with a silent Gunner beside me, I stood on the other side of the counter in a well-lit automobile dealership and felt like I'd taken a misstep forward and stumbled off a cliff. "You mean it'll be expensive to repair her," I suggested. "How much are we talking? Five hundred dollars? Six hundred? More?"

The human glanced at me once with pity in his eyes, then returned his attention to Gunner. "For fifty bucks, we'll take it to the crusher. Or, if you're looking for a new set of wheels, Joe here can likely give you five percent off any new vehicle on the lot."

Joe nodded from a nearby counter, exuding the same smarmy pleasantry shared by salesmen everywhere. But that wasn't why my hackles rose. Instead, I tensed as Gunner hesitated, clearly wishing to replace my vehicle with something more reliable but at the same time well aware that I'd never let Old Red—and the freedom she represented—slip away without a fight.

Perhaps it was my flaring nostrils that won him over. Whatever the reason, after only a millisecond of internal debate, Gunner backed me up. "How much to repair the vehicle we brought in yesterday?"

"Two."

I wanted that to mean two hundred, but I knew from the way the mechanic twisted up his face that he meant a whole lot more. Two *thousand?* At the same time, my phone chimed and I glanced down, noting an incoming call.

From Kira. From a sister who usually texted, saying it was too time consuming to actually *talk* with me.

Reality was literally calling. So, caving to the inevitable, I told Gunner, "You deal with this." Then I stepped away to answer the phone.

Behind me, the werewolf dealt with the car situation in the exact way I didn't want him to. "You—make that discount ten percent and we'll take the best car on the lot."

"The *best* car?" I could see dollar signs rolling through the salesman's head as he considered a commission on what was bound to be the most expensive car he had available rather than the best. Meanwhile, I could feel my own debt piling back up like walls around me, just months after I'd last wiggled my way out from under its weight.

But Kira was speaking into my ear now, her words running together in a way that made hairs rise along the back of my neck. "Oyo wasn't here when I woke up this morning," she said. "Tank and Allen aren't answering their cell phones. And there are scary noises coming from the direction of the Green. What do I do next?"

It looked like I had far greater problems than losing Old Red.

Chapter 21

"**M**aybe you should try calling Tank?" I offered three hours later as we sped along the final leg of our journey toward home. I was driving the shiny new sedan that was superior to Old Red in every way...at least from Gunner's point of view.

Not that we'd had time to argue about his vehicular decision. Instead, Gunner was trying to figure out what had happened at clan central during our absence, a task made significantly more difficult when everyone refused to answer their phones. Even Kira's texts had transitioned from vague to outright evasive as the afternoon faded closer and closer toward night.

Adding to our stress levels, there were werewolves who didn't belong scattered all along the drive home. First, the scent of fur had surrounded us at a service station well into Atwood territory where we'd stopped to fill my new car with gas. Old Red would have required refueling long before then, making me grudgingly admit that the new car's improved gas efficiency would save me money in the long run—money I wouldn't have to ask Gunner for.

Still, I refused to name our current ride, instead keeping my attention riveted on our surroundings. Sure enough, a flicker of movement out of the corner of my eye an hour later had resolved into a trio of unfamiliar wolves racing down the side of the interstate as if they owned the place.

"Not ours," Gunner had confirmed when I glanced in his direction. But we hadn't stopped to investigate. We couldn't afford to get sidetracked when the replies from Kira had stopped arriving by that point.

No wonder Gunner couldn't quite manage to come up with human words as he growled out a curt reply to my suggestion to call his most trusted lieutenant. *Of course*, he'd already tried Tank half a dozen times over the course of our travels. That went without saying. But it was better that he beat his head against the cell phone than turn four-legged and feral as I drove.

Then we were there, the unmarked driveway disappearing into darkness beneath the glowering tree canopy. Gunner's hand—almost a paw—landed atop my arm as I prepared to flick on the headlights. "No," he ordered. "Park here."

Obediently, I pulled over and shut off the engine. Rolled down my window and listened to the night. It was quieter than it should have been, as if wildlife had fled in the face of a terrifying predator—like the wolf who now appeared by my side.

Gunner hadn't bothered to undress before shifting, and he wriggled out of his clothes as he stepped across my lap. The boxer shorts landing on my knee might have been intimate under other circumstances. As it was, I knew Gunner was merely angling for the window so he could make his escape.

"Wait," I told him...and he *did* wait just long enough for me to crack open the car door so we could disembark together. With a whisper of magic, my star ball materialized into my hand then solidified into the reassuring mass of a sword's hilt.

At last, I was armed and ready to take off down the road at a run.

Only Gunner halted our forward motion a second time. Taking my left hand into his jaws as gently as if I was made of tissue paper, he pulled me off the road, through a hanging curtain of ivy...and onto a trail I hadn't known existed before today.

Which would have been no surprise if our move-in day had been my first introduction to Atwood territory. But Kira and I had come here at least half a dozen times over the last few months since Gunner had become the alpha in residence. I'd run nearby trails with Tank and Allen...and many times with Gunner himself. The fact I'd never been in this vegetation-shrouded tunnel suggested I'd been deliberately left out of the loop.

Is that how mates treat each other? Ignoring the twinge in my gut at the omission, I followed Gunner through the tunnel without protesting the past. There was no time to mull over hurt feelings when the setting sun made silence from my sister more ominous with every step.

After that, we traveled for several minutes in silence before Gunner stopped so abruptly that I almost stepped on his feet. I reached forward to catch my balance, steadying myself on his furry rump...

...Then my fingers clenched into fists as I heard what had stopped him. Outside our tunnel, the air rang with the clanging of swords.

NOW WE WERE RUNNING as best we could within the confined tunnel. And as the trail split in two before us, Gunner, to my distress, turned away from rather than toward the much louder battle sounds.

"But..." I started, then decided to trust him. And was glad I had when, barely a minute later, we emerged from the trees just behind the roiling melee.

This was the same spot of the ill-fated bacon breakfast. The same spot where Edward and I made our differences worse rather than better as we fought. So I wasn't entirely surprised to come out of the tunnel into fighting...I was merely shocked at the extent of the pitched battle made up of angry wolves.

It appeared as if the entire pack was present, the haze of sulfur so strong it nearly made me choke. All of them were human, too, as they sliced at their friends with wicked metal blades.

As I watched, Tank—the level-headed lawyer who used words as his weapon—slashed twin knives at a female I couldn't remember the name of but who'd attended my spur-of-the-moment swordsmanship class the day before. No milquetoast, his opponent grinned ferociously and fought back with a sword that looked remarkably like one of the advanced-level training blades I'd packed into a duffel. The only problem was, she'd removed the protective foam intended to shield the tip.

The female lunged forward with more grace than I remembered her being capable of. And, sure enough, her sword raised a streak of blood along Tank's forearm before the latter managed to knock the blow aside.

Now that I saw them together, in fact, I was relatively sure this same female had been flirting with Tank just a few weeks earlier. Which would have been fine if they'd only been sparring rather than, apparently, battling to the death.

Something was seriously wrong here. But all I could think was—*Kira, Kira, where is Kira?* Spinning, I ignored battling pack mates in search of the teenager I knew would be somewhere in their midst.

And there she was, on a picnic blanket in the center of the disaster, bouncing with excitement as Sakurako held her in place with one gnarled hand.

This was so wrong I didn't know where to begin chipping away at the problem. "Gunner," I started, speaking to the wolf vibrating with anger beside me.

Unfortunately, at that moment the battling shifters took note of my presence. And rather than offering the real or feigned respect they usually showed me, one in particular shed his facade of pleasantry and leapt away from his current opponent so he could threaten me instead.

Edward's face contorted with rage as he raised a massive ax over his head with both hands while roaring like a berserker. And all I thought was, *Gunner will have no doubt of Edward's allegiances now.*

Chapter 22

My sword was useless against an ax. But, luckily, my weaponry was magical. So instead of stabbing the attacking werewolf, I flattened my star ball out into a shield as the tremendous wedge fell toward me from above.

The weight, when the ax struck, was excruciating, the star ball's magical-yet-material gripping straps reverberating painfully within my hands. But my energy-infused armor held. And I breathed more deeply as it became apparent that Edward's attack would do no more than bruise my skin.

Gunner, on the other hand, was enraged by his underling's disloyalty. His ominous growl was nearly too quiet to hear above my own panting, but the alpha's scent promised that Edward might not live to see the light of another day.

I wasn't particularly thrilled with Edward either. But we'd all regret it if Gunner tore out Edward's throat in a fit of rage without first understanding what had happened to the rest of the pack.

So my next parry involved diving between the two shifters, clunking the alpha's chin with my knee as a mild hint that now might be a good time to take a calming breath. Gunner growled then whimpered, clearly getting the message. But Edward was the one who dropped his ax and stood dazed and blinking between us, his brow furrowed and mouth gaping as he strained to come up with words.

It was almost as if a kitsune had stolen his blood and used it to force him into the prior fighting...then had lost interest and left the male cold and confused. "What...?" Edward started, oblivious to the fact that yet another pack mate was rushing toward us with edged metal glinting. Or, rather, was rushing toward Edward, never mind that I was pretty sure the younger shifter was his sister's son.

In reaction, my star ball shrunk, stretched, glistened into swordishness. Edward might be annoying, but he was an Atwood pack mate and I was bound to protect his life. So I pivoted, retreated, then lunged toward the new attacker. And now Edward was picking up his ax to join me...even as the blond werewolf fumbled and cut himself on his own blade.

Cut himself while trying for one of the easiest sword-fighting maneuvers imaginable. What was the male doing wielding a weapon if he didn't know how to fight with one?

It was an easy matter to swipe my own sword sideways and send the younger male's weapon skittering off into the dark. Harder was managing not to injure the shifter's unshielded body as he came at me with bare hands.

Then someone shouted from behind me. The hairs on my neck prickled, and I whirled away from a werewolf who I suspected wouldn't manage to do more than scratch me with human nails.

Because something had shifted. Something was different....

There. Not where the shout had come from, but in the opposite direction where the cluster of werewolves was more densely packed together. An arm rose above the crowd. A long dark shape arched back then flew directly toward us.

The tip glinted—a knife point affixed to a wooden handle creating a homemade javelin. And, unaware that he stood at the terminus of its trajectory, Gunner raised his muzzle in preparation for howling his pack back into line.

THERE WAS NO TIME FOR warning, for magic, for anything. I was too far away from Gunner, having become separated while preventing him from tearing out the throat of his own pack mate.

But Edward was close enough to save him. Edward, who hated me but whose gaze latched onto mine at just the perfect moment. Whose eyes flicked toward the falling javelin in an attempt to understand the horror on my face.

Edward didn't hesitate before throwing himself between his alpha and the descending danger. The thunk of knife hitting flesh was sickening. The wheeze of air erupting from a lung, not through a trachea but out between ribcage and punctured skin, made my own breath seize up in response.

While I stood frozen, the blond nephew dropped to his knees beside Edward, already keening out his sorrow. "No! Uncle! *No!*"

Even dying, Edward somehow found the energy to pat his nephew's hand consolingly. Meanwhile, his gaze once again latched onto mine. *"Protect our pack,"* he ordered, the words soundless yet the motion of his lips visible in the near darkness.

Then Gunner was shifting to replace the grief-stricken nephew, the battlefield growing silent as the pack leader's hands pressed hard against the gaping wound on the older male's chest. The javelin had gone straight through and out the other side cleanly—and who would have been able to do that from a hundred feet distant without practicing day and night?

Whoever had done it, however they'd done it, Edward wasn't getting back up from this injury. And Gunner accepted that fact with the grace of a clan leader thinking of his larger responsibilities rather than about only one member of his pack.

"You have my gratitude," the alpha started. Electricity from shifting werewolves filled the air even as an undulating howl rose up from dozens of shifters who had, one moment earlier, been battling against their family and friends. "Go in peace into the afterlife."

"Promise." Edward's gaze met mine rather than responding to his alpha, his eyes already starting to glaze over with death. He wasn't even looking at me, I realized. Was instead peering over my left shoulder, as if he'd lost track of his surroundings and was only hanging on long enough to hear my response.

Gunner glanced backwards in reaction, raising his eyebrows when he saw I was on the receiving end of Edward's mouthed admonition. Then he scooted sideways, making room for me by the dying werewolf's side.

"I promise," I murmured to both of them, not certain what, exactly, I was agreeing to. I had no time to press Edward for further information however. Because, with one last wheeze from the hole in his chest cavity, my clearest enemy within the clan subsided into death.

Chapter 23

"I'll take care of this," Gunner told me, his voice curt as he strode away to trail his hands across the heads of panting shifters. They were clearly in need of a pack leader's attention, so I didn't complain about the tone of his voice. Not when I had a pressing problem of my own to attend to—Kira standing hand-in-hand with our grandmother, both fully surrounded by a ring of men wielding swords.

These were the humans our grandmother had treated like puppies yesterday, but they didn't appear particularly gentle at the moment. Instead, they held their weapons in exactly the proper manner. Loosely en garde and ready to slice into anyone who looked at their charges with the wrong gleam in their eye.

Despite their clear training, however, I approached without hesitation, stopping just far enough away from the closest male so my sword could meet his advance should he decide to attack. But that was all the attention I gave to the humans. Instead, I peered over the guard's shoulder at the old woman in their midst.

She was still small and still wrinkled. But—if I guessed right—she was also the impetus of the recent battle that had caused at least one werewolf's death. And Sakurako made no effort to explain her actions. Instead, the elderly kitsune greeted me with a single word.

"Granddaughter."

Well, if she wasn't going to explain herself, then I'd deal with the only thing she held that I still cared about. "Kira, come here," I demanded, knowing it wouldn't be so easy to get my sister safely out from behind the ring of swords.

I expected the males to stop her from passing between them. Or, perhaps, for my grandmother to finally show her true colors and use kitsune magic to hold Kira in place. Instead, it was Kira herself who planted her feet and refused me. "Mai, chill," she answered with yet another teenagerly roll of the eyes.

So I'd have to cut my way through the swordsmen to reach her. A matter made slightly more realistic when two wolves bumped their shoulders into my hips. Tank and Allen—I could smell them without looking downward. Unlike the rest of Gunner's pack mates, I would trust these two with my—or rather, with my sister's—life.

So I didn't pause as I strode forward, ignoring the way five swords swung toward me in tandem as they prepared to hinder my approach. The bodyguards were almost too pretty to be fighters, their perfect faces so similar I couldn't help thinking they'd been chosen not for skill but rather for looks.

I couldn't count on that, however. Couldn't count on anything except the star-ball sword that was now raised between me and danger, plus the two wolves standing firmly at my back. Three against five wasn't terrible...but the battle would be dicey with Kira unprotected and open to enemy attack.

As if hearing those thoughts, my sister snorted, wrenched her hand free of our grandmother's, then slipped between the guards as easily as if they were trees planted in a grassy meadow. "Mai, I *told* you, they're protecting *me*."

She hadn't actually said that, but I was the one failing to listen now. Because I held my breath as Kira padded forward, waiting for someone to restrain the departing child.

Except...all five guards plus my wily kitsune grandmother did nothing. No, that wasn't quite true. One guard scooted sideways to give Kira space to pass unhindered. Another bowed ever so subtly while, behind them, our grandmother merely smiled as if this had been her intention all along.

"Thanks for the help, guys," Kira called back over one shoulder. Then she was beside me while Allen shifted upwards to grab onto her before she could slip away from us.

"Ow!" Kira complained, attempting to shrug free of the protective grip of the werewolf. And this time the armed humans hardened, took a step forward...then halted at the subtlest clearing of my grandmother's throat.

It really did appear that these swordsmen had been charged with protecting Kira rather than with menacing her. Still, "Take her home," I murmured. And Tank and Allen obeyed me, drawing Kira away from the danger, the latter two-legged and the former still in the shape of his wolf.

As for myself, I firmed up my stance between the strangers and my retreating sister, fully expecting complaint from the swordsmen or from the woman who had told me to call her by a pet name the day before. Instead, the old woman cackled, pressing through her guard just as Kira had done moments earlier. She didn't stop when she'd breached her guards, however. Instead Sakurako just kept coming until she could reach up and cup my face with crinkly fingers that felt unbearably cold against my over-heated skin.

"Now that you've called off your dogs, granddaughter," she told me, "perhaps we can finally finish our little talk."

"YOU WANT TO TALK?" I barely restrained myself from physically shaking sense back into the woman who swore she was my grandmother but acted like someone intent upon tearing everything I cared about apart. "We have nothing left to talk about. You asked if I was willing to give up Oyo and...."

"Stop." Sakurako held a hand palm-out between us, and I wasn't quite rude enough to talk over her. After all, she was old and was one of only two surviving relatives. So I obeyed the gesture and gave her space in which to speak.

Only the old woman didn't. Instead, she nodded at her guards, sending all except one striding away from us into the darkness. Then, once her final lackey started folding the picnic blanket, she slipped her fingers around my elbow and led us away from the carnage of the battlefield.

"I misunderstood your affection for these werewolves," she said after a moment, and I could tell she rarely admitted to having been wrong. "This is not my work, but I could have stopped it if I'd made an effort. Next time, I'll think more deeply about what you might have wished."

It wasn't quite an apology and I definitely didn't believe in her supposed lack of involvement. Still, I didn't tear my arm out of her grasp and storm away into the night. "What do you want?" I asked instead, my tone not quite cordial but not so antagonistic that the male now trotting behind us dropped Sakurako's picnic paraphernalia and drew his sword.

"I want a chance to explain to you about the larger world you are a part of," my grandmother answered quickly. "Oyo—yes, I want Oyo also. But I was premature to set a deadline on that decision. I know you well enough by now to see that once you understand the repercussions, you will make the proper choice."

She thought I was wrapped around her little finger just like her guards and—apparently—Kira were. She assumed that acting like a doddering old woman would win my affection and garner my regard.

But I wasn't stupid enough to be fooled a second time. So I merely shook my head. "My decision is made, Sakurako. I don't trust you around my friends or around Kira. You know my answer. I want you out of clan central before..."

"What if I made a promise?" Once again, my grandmother had spoken over me. And, once again, I closed my mouth and allowed her to speak. "I swear to protect, not harm, everyone you care about for the next twenty-four hours. Is that good enough to buy one more day to change your mind?"

It wouldn't have been if she'd been a werewolf or a human. But I could feel Sakurako's kitsune oath binding us together and placing her in my debt as she spoke.

Plus, I remembered how carefully she'd guarded Kira. How easily she'd released my sister back into my care once I demanded the youngster be returned to me.

And yet.... *Now that you've called off your dogs, granddaughter.* The words rolled through my mind in belated warning. Sakurako was protecting my "dogs" only because she wanted something from me, not because she thought they deserved protection for their own sake.

Still, I trusted the kitsune oath to keep the pack together for twenty-four hours. And I was also getting the distinct impression that my familial stubbornness may have seen its source in Sakurako's veins.

So I accepted defeat gracefully. Bowing my head, I caved to her offer. "Tomorrow we will speak again, Sobo. Tonight, I need to help my pack lick their wounds."

Chapter 24

Only, the pack didn't need me. Or so I gathered when I reached the far end of the Green and saw the way wolves encircled Gunner in a tight cluster. They were just standing there, over a hundred furry bodies all touching their neighbors with chins, necks, and noses. And, even though I couldn't feel it, I could imagine the rebuilding of shattered bonds taking place before me, the magic of pack recreating what had recently been lost.

This was the sort of thing a fox shouldn't stick her nose into. Just watching them made me feel small, cold, and sad. So I backtracked to the scene of the battle, intent upon doing at least a little good before falling into my bed and calling it a night.

Because if Sakurako was to be believed and the recent fight hadn't been instigated by a kitsune, that meant a member of that cluster of shifters had murderously thrown a homemade javelin at his or her alpha. But who would do that to Gunner? Edward was the one who'd shared the most overt disapproval of the alpha's governing processes...and yet Edward had also been the one who'd leapt to Gunner's defense without regard for the safety of his own skin.

I winced, remembering the way the javelin had struck with so much force it slid all the way through the deceased male's body. No wonder the weapon was now lying abandoned on the ground even though Edward had been carried away in preparation for some sort of werewolf farewell to the dead.

"Haven't you done enough already?"

My hand skittered away from the bloody broomstick that made up the weapon's handle, the ball of my hand nicking itself on the knife lashed to the end as haste flubbed my retreat. But, despite the pain, I remained crouched on the grass beside the weapon. After all, Elizabeth's father had died less than an hour earlier. She deserved the courtesy of the upper hand.

Plus, Gunner was close enough that he could be here almost immediately if my awkward posture left me open to attack by this werewolf. So I let Elizabeth's words hang between us for several seconds, then I answered the question she hadn't asked.

"I'm trying to figure out who killed your father," I told her, leaning down further until my nose nearly touched the spot where a hand would have clutched the broomstick while throwing it. Unfortunately, it was impossible to pick out identifying aromas through the coating of blood smeared across the handle, so I soon settled back on my heels in regret.

"You won't find any scent there," Elizabeth told me. And for half a second I thought she was admitting to having been involved in her own father's murder. But then something long and heavy landed on the ground beside me. A throwing stick with a protrusion just big enough for the hollowed out end of the broomstick to fit over—no wonder the javelin had flown so forcefully. And when I leaned down to sniff this second item, I found no scent at all along its length.

A plastic grocery bag half wrapped around the end answered the question of why Elizabeth's odor hadn't rubbed off on the wooden handle while she carried it across the field. But shouldn't even gloved fingers have left some scent, whether leather or plastic? I was pretty sure they should have, which meant the killer had used a trick like the scent-reducing compound I'd sprayed on my own flesh two nights earlier to prevent Gunner from smelling the fact that I'd been manhandled by another wolf.

"You promised my father that you would protect the Atwoods," Elizabeth continued. And for the first time I heard something other than anger in her voice. She'd lost a parent this evening. Of course she was traumatized. I wanted to stand up and hug her, but I knew she'd resist the embrace.

"I did," I said simply.

"Then do what you promised." For half a second, the young woman reeked of fur and electricity. She needed to shift, needed to accept the unity Gunner was offering the rest of the pack.

Instead, she kicked the throwing stick lightly with one blood-stained sneaker. "Find out who killed my father and prevent it from happening again. Or solve the problem the easy way and get out of our pack."

I WAS HALFWAY BACK to my cottage, intent upon calling it a night, when a voice in the darkness stopped me. "Mai-san." Whirling, my hand was on my sword hilt even before I made out the shape of one of the five human swordsmen who'd recently dogged my grandmother's footsteps.

Just a few minutes earlier, this human had appeared ominous and forbidding as he trapped my sister within a ring of swords. Now, though, his body language was entirely the opposite as he deferred to me not only in posture but also with the honorific tacked onto the end of my name.

The Atwood pack wasn't interested in including me in their rituals this evening, but my grandmother's lackey had clearly taken the time to search me out. And as I noted his obvious Japanese heritage, I wondered if the reason might be shared blood.

"I came to explain, to speak with you," he said when curiosity held me in place. Then he proved himself clever by getting straight to the point. "Sakurako-sama has had a difficult life, so she builds up walls to protect herself. It takes some getting used to."

"Yeah, like eating raw fish." The words flowed out of me before I could stop them. But, to my surprise, the human laughed rather than taking offense.

"I'm Yuki," he said, offering a bow but no comment about my assessment of his employer. "Would it be too forward of me to ask if you plan to accept Sakurako-sama's invitation tomorrow? I hope you will choose to come."

"Invitation?" I'd gotten the impression my grandmother merely wanted to speak with me. But Yuki made this sound like an event rather than a simple conversation.

"She didn't explain." Yuki laughed quietly, the chuckle warming me due to its similarity to my mother's laughter when I was very young. "Sakurako-sama believes everything is on a need-to-know basis. But this, I think, you need to know."

We were walking as we talked, back toward my cottage. And I hesitated ten feet from my door, intrigued by this possible family member...but not enough that I wanted to invite him inside.

"I'm all ears," I offered. Then, as Yuki cocked his head in confusion, I realized that his stilted speech probably meant English was his second language. So—"I'm listening," I offered instead.

"The mistress wants to show you your heritage," Yuki told me, accepting my explanation gracefully. And when I didn't interject a comment, he elaborated as best he could. "It's not my place to tell you where she wishes to take you or what she plans to show you there. But I'll be coming tomorrow and would be honored if you traveled by my side."

Traveled. This wasn't a decision I could make tonight while exhausted and lonely. "I'll see you tomorrow," I answered noncommittally. Then, bowing a farewell to Yuki, I entered my cottage alone.

Chapter 25

O r I thought I was alone until a voice rang out from deeper within the darkened living room. "So you're the kitsune." Clearly, lack of lights meant very little when denning with wolves.

I tensed, prepared for another ultimatum like the one I'd recently had dumped on me by Elizabeth. Only...this was no Atwood. I was pretty sure everyone in Gunner's pack was either being soothed by their alpha or was protecting my sister. Meanwhile, the air within my cottage was redolent with the unfamiliar scent of bitter almond, suggesting my questioner was someone I'd never met before.

Someone I'd never met but who just happened to know my identity. Ignoring my racing heart, I flicked on the light switch as if my world wasn't crumbling down around me.

"What's a kit sunny?" I asked, purposefully mispronouncing the name of my own kind while assessing my uninvited visitor out of the corner of one eye.

Despite being in another shifter's territory, the broad, menacing stranger lounged on my plush sofa as if he owned the place, legs splayed and arms spread so he took up enough room for three people or more. I didn't smell any fur or electricity to go along with the power pose, but something told me not to turn my back on this werewolf.

I did so anyway. Walked past him without waiting for an answer then padded down the hall in search of the sister who should have been asleep in her bed. The air didn't smell like Tank, Allen, or Kira, however, suggesting the trio had made a pitstop before obeying my order. Oyo on the other hand could pop out at any moment directly into the jaws of the strange, bitter-almond-scented wolf....

In an effort to prevent that eventuality, I crouched down to peer into the darkness beneath my bedstead, stretching my fingers into the hole in the wall. When Kira had called to tell me the redheaded kitsune was missing, I'd assumed Oyo had heard about my grandmother's arrival then dug herself in deeper. But the gap in the drywall was both empty and cold.

"I'm speaking to you, fox."

Head under the bed, I'd missed the stranger sneaking up behind me. But I couldn't miss the way he dragged me out of the darkness by my hips. Hard hands on my shoulders slammed me up against the wall before I could make a comment on being manhandled, and I silently berated myself for turning my back on someone much larger and stronger than myself.

Aloud, though, I disavowed all understanding of the situation. "What's wrong with you?" I blustered. "And what do you mean by calling me a fox?"

The shifter silenced me the easy way, backhanding me so hard my head slammed into the drywall. Darkness tried to claim me as his hot breath flowed across my stinging cheek. And I tried without success to think of a way out of the situation that didn't involve creating a magical dagger to thrust into my opponent's gut.

I can't show what I am unless I'm ready to kill him. The knowledge chilled me even as it narrowed my options to...well, none.

Meanwhile, the male who held me began speaking, his voice so cold I shivered despite every effort to appear impervious. "Let me spell it out for you, kitsune," he murmured. "I'm an enforcer." At my blank look, he sighed and elaborated. "I decide on life or death for werewolves...and all who come in contact with them."

"No, Gunner is the pack leader. His word is law." This part wasn't bluster. I thoroughly believed that fact or I never would have brought Kira to live in Atwood clan central.

"A *werewolf* would know that is true only of problems that don't threaten the neighbors." My opponent dropped me so abruptly I slid down onto my butt rather than regaining my footing. "But enough about me. I want to hear about you."

This wasn't a threat—this was a warning. So I did the only thing I could think of. I raised my hand to my mouth as if in terror. And, surreptitiously, I licked up a stray droplet of Edward's blood.

THE PACK BONDS FLARED to life so quickly that I almost thought they'd always been there. This was no time for analyzing magic, however. Instead, as the enforcer dragged me upright, I ignored his muttered demands and tugged as hard as I could on the solid rope that led from me to my not-quite-mate.

"Gunner!"

"Isn't here to help you, kitsune." A fist slammed into my stomach and I lost my ability to verbalize. Instead, I strove to send the pack leader an image of what he'd be walking into if he raced here to help me. I needed his assistance, but it was too dangerous for him to walk into this ambush blind.

And Gunner must have heard me. Both heard and understood me. Because images now flowed back the other way in answer. Images of a gathering of alpha-leaning werewolves, the mass of them telling this stranger what to do.

So, an enforcer was some kind of regional sheriff? I wasn't entirely sure I understood what Gunner was trying to tell me. Rather than providing time for questions, however, he managed to send through two words loud and clear.

"Get away."

Good idea. I both wanted to laugh at the obviousness of Gunner's suggestion and to vomit from the sharp agony spiking through my gut where the enforcer had driven his fist. Instead of doing either, I let my legs crumple a second time...then I dove between the enforcer's knees as he allowed me to drop.

Only my opponent was fast and smart and ready for me. His foot came down on my spine as I slid past him. Then I was supine on the floor while once again struggling to regain my breath.

"These are simple questions, kitsune." His words seemed to come from the other end of a long tunnel, and I couldn't have answered even if I'd wanted to with carpet fibers embedded in my mouth. "Which werewolves do you manipulate?" he demanded, sending my mind off on a tangent of guesswork.

Did kitsunes have a pattern of behavior, insinuating themselves into werewolf clan centrals and tearing down not only that pack but the neighbors also? Was that why Sakurako had come here, what had riled up non-Atwood wolves enough to send this enforcer to find me? Was that fate what Oyo was hiding from?

"This is your last chance," the enforcer growled as he flipped me over. There was a knife in his hand now, I noted. A knife that hovered so close above my left eyeball that I couldn't focus on the tip poised to impale me.

It was finally time to shift, I decided. I had nothing left to lose and everything to gain....

Only Gunner leapt through the door in a whirlwind of cold air and enraged werewolf before I could get my magic together. He was mostly human—kinda human. Human enough to bellow instructions in my direction before diving onto the enforcer in the full skin of his wolf.

"Kira is on her way to your grandmother's. Join her and flee as far and as fast as you're able."

And even though the enforcer laughed, frost spreading out from the stranger's feet as if he was as magical as I was, I did what Gunner suggested. I turned tail and fled from the battleground that had recently been a welcoming home.

Chapter 26

Kira had to be my top priority. I knew this even as the pack bond informed me that Gunner was fighting...and losing.

Meanwhile, shifters streamed past in the opposite direction, rushing to assist their alpha as the pack bond alerted them to Gunner's fate. But they piled up in the doorway, frozen by the enforcer's dominance and unable to set a single step inside.

Gunner, for his part, was being shredded and battered. Blood stung his/my eyeball as I experienced the pain right alongside him, and he limped to avoid putting pressure on his front left foot.

Still, Gunner fought with all the abandon of a werewolf protecting his partner even though I'd never overtly chosen him. *"Hurry,"* he suggested, the word warm in my belly. And I blinked back tears that blocked my vision, using my second-strongest tether as a guide leading me toward family and escape.

"The neighbors are gathering." Tank appeared out of nowhere with Kira wide-eyed and panting behind him. "We have to get you out of here before they block the exits. Did the enforcer see you shift?"

"No." That much, at least, I'd done correctly. But—"I can't find Oyo. If she shows up in fox form, what will happen to Gunner then?"

Tank didn't speak, but his grim silence was its own sort of answer. Then we were in front of my grandmother's camper, the massive bulk of it menacing in the dark.

And for the first time since leaving my cottage, I hesitated. I'd parted from these near strangers with no real conclusion earlier, didn't trust any of them despite my grandmother's recent oath.

Kira, on the other hand, had no such reservations. "Sobo!" Her voice—and her pounding fists—broke the silence. Lights flared on inside the RV a millisecond before Yuki answered the door.

It's going to be alright. Despite the pain I felt every time Gunner accepted a blow that was meant for my ribcage, Yuki's appearance gave me hope. Sure enough, the human took only one look at our faces before ushering us inside the vehicle. Meanwhile, the rest of Sakurako's entourage flowed out around us, began working in seamless synchrony to crank in the RV's popped-out sides.

"The best route away is east," Tank informed me from beyond the still-open doorway. He wasn't coming with us. None of these werewolves would leave clan central while their alpha was engaged in a deadly battle.

Or maybe I'd misgauged the loyalty of Gunner's pack mates. Because a dark shape pushed past Gunner's most loyal underling, materializing into Becky with her bloodling pup cradled in both arms.

Cradled...then extended towards me. "Take him. Please," she begged, ignoring everyone else as she ran halfway up the stairs and attempted to thrust the sleeping pup into my arms. The female was terrified, hesitated only long enough to glance back over one shoulder before descending into a litany of promises I knew she couldn't keep.

"I'll do anything for you if you'll protect him. And he'll help you. Werewolf blood is powerful. Curly, tell them you want them to take your blood if they need it. That you won't fight against a cut."

The puppy hadn't been sleeping, I realized. He'd been doing the only thing he could to help—keeping himself silent and still.

Now, as his body slid away from his mother's and up against my sweatshirt, he didn't attempt to reverse the flow of his own motion. Instead, he peered up at me with dark eyes full of understanding, then he nodded his lupine head.

But, of course, despite his cuteness, Curly wasn't a puppy. He was a young werewolf, well aware of what would happen if the Atwood pack was overrun. I wasn't exactly sure what that awfulness would consist of. And yet, given the slights Becky had faced from supposedly friendly shifters, I was able to take a wild guess.

"You come too," I demanded, pulling Becky up beside me. But she resisted and I had to release my hold so Curly wouldn't fall to the ground.

"No, I can't leave my pack," the other female murmured. For a millisecond, her hand extended as if to pet—or regain—Curly. But then the gesture aborted. And without a word of farewell to her only offspring, she turned on her heel and sprinted back toward the cottage where Gunner fought.

TANK FOLLOWED HIS PACK mate, leaving me alone with two kitsunes, a bloodling pup, and five male humans. To my surprise, Sakurako slipped into the driver's seat, taking the curves far faster than I would have been able to without risking a spill.

Beside me, Kira cradled Curly, the pup so silent I thought at first that he was soundly sleeping. But, no, Curly was merely feeling what I was feeling—that brittle breaking in his middle as he was spirited away from every other member of the Atwood pack.

Because my own connection to Gunner had begun to falter as the distance increased between us. I could no longer see what the enforcer was doing back in our cottage, only felt fists and teeth cutting into my mate as a dull, distant ache.

Then even that bodily contact faded. And I gasped, unable to breathe around the thought that Gunner might have faded right along with it. I'd made the wrong decision, choosing Kira over my partner....

Yuki was the one who noted my silent anguish, who knelt before me and clutched five of my frozen fingers in ten of his own. "We'll make it out of here," he promised...even as Sakurako slammed on the brakes and abruptly shut off both engine and headlights.

Pay attention, I told myself, shutting Gunner's fate away in a tiny box shrouded in black ribbons. I'd chosen my family over our romantic partnership; it was time to ensure neither Kira nor Sakurako was caught in the undertow now.

To that end, I scooted around Yuki and peered out the windshield into darkness. There were snowflakes in the air despite the fact that it was only early October. Snowflakes that settled on the glass and might soon stick to the soil.

How easy would it be to follow our trail with a blanket of snow on the ground to turn tracks into billboards? Our enemies wouldn't even need a predator's nose.

"They're ahead. A quarter of a mile," the old woman said tersely. She glanced in my direction, raised one brow. "Your werewolf didn't know what he was talking about. I hope you have another way out of these woods."

And, as I peered at the brand new yet abandoned vehicle Gunner and I had arrived in not long ago, I realized that I did. It seemed disloyal to reveal Gunner's tunnel to strangers. Still, would it even matter that Sakurako knew about the secret passageway if the Atwood pack leader might already be dead?

"Mai?" Kira's voice was so small I barely heard her, but it slammed me back into the present and out of the abyss of loss. I'd resolved to protect my sister above all others. So I'd lead us to safety...then, later, I could fall apart.

"This way," I told them, descending from the vehicle so I could lead two kitsunes and five humans away into the forest. Curly I clutched to my chest as much to soothe me as to warm him. Meanwhile, behind us, one of the males sprayed an aerosol of de-scenting compound across the ground to eliminate our trail.

Chapter 27

I was so shaken by thoughts of Gunner that it took a solid minute for the implications of that spray can to sink into my conscious thought processes. But then I flinched as the male in question slipped past my arm and into the tunnel I'd just pointed out, his possible identity making me want nothing more than to turn tail and run.

Was this the male who'd tried to kill Gunner? Who'd thrown a javelin without imbuing it with his aroma? If so, I'd been looking at this issue from all the wrong angles...or, rather, I'd thrown in my lot with the enemy when I'd opted to include Sakurako and her lackeys in my escape.

"It's standard issue." Yuki was the only one who noticed my hesitation, the only one who didn't slip beneath the overhanging greenery and follow our companions inside. "Werewolves are our greatest e—" He paused, glanced at Curly still clutched in my arms, then chose a different word. "Danger. So we carry these spray cans to cover our footsteps, to protect ourselves from attack."

Sure enough, a similar canister appeared between his fingers...which didn't make me particularly inclined to trust him more than his friend. But my grandmother reemerged from behind the veil of plants at that moment, grabbed my shirtsleeve, and yanked me inside.

"Shift," she demanded, her word lacking alpha compulsion but nonetheless spurring everyone around her into action. Kira's clothes dropped into a pile along with the males' cell phones, then my sister shimmered into fox form even as two different humans sprayed the pile of discarded possessions to make it harder for werewolves to find us using either biology or technology.

So maybe Yuki was right. Maybe there were dozens of people out there carrying similar sprays meant to confuse werewolf nostrils. I'd stay alert, but my choice of allies had already been set in stone when I abandoned my mate.

Still, I didn't obey Sakurako, merely stood my ground and stated my case for remaining human. "I'm not leaving Curly." I couldn't carry the pup in fox form, and he'd last about three minutes under his own volition at a sprint.

Sakurako shook her head in answer then turned her back to slither out of her nightgown. Like Kira, the old woman glowed as she shifted, but her transition was more of a supernova than the twinkle of a distant star. I rubbed my eyes, trying to make sense of the vision. Sakurako's luminous white fur gleamed in the near darkness. And was night playing tricks on me or did she really boast multiple tails?

I only had a second to stare at the strange kitsune, however, before tires on gravel heralded the arrival of enemy werewolves. We'd left the RV blocking the roadway, so it was inevitable our enemies would begin searching momentarily. We had to be out of earshot before that happened. Was I really ready to endanger our entire party for the sake of one bloodling wolf?

Curly whined, peering up at me. Then Yuki was at my shoulder, arms outstretched. "I'll carry him." He glanced toward the white fox, already receding into the darkness, then told me: "I'll put his life before mine, I promise."

And Yuki must have had kitsune blood somewhere inside him, because his words came out oath-like and binding. That was exactly the confirmation I was waiting for. So even as the first car door creaked open, I relinquished my burden and fell down into the form of my fox.

WE RAN FOR EONS. OUTSIDE the tunnel, snow fell harder and faster, the fraction that filtered down through interwoven trees and shrubs not quite sufficient to slow our footsteps. I'd never thought kitsunes could control the weather, but it seemed like a strange coincidence that such a dramatic snowstorm had blown in out of nowhere at the exact moment we started fleeing from hunting wolves.

Because I'd been wrong—the snow helped rather than hindered us. It muffled our scent and covered our tracks even as we fled through the network of tunnels some long-dead werewolf had created out of bushes and trees.

Our enemies didn't give up the chase, however, even though passage through the forest had to be much more difficult outside our vegetative pathway. Instead, their howls were terrifyingly close at first, then only a little more distant when trees laden with both leaves and snow began thundering to the ground and further blocking our pursuers' paths.

One huge trunk in particular smashed into the tunnel behind us, making Kira squeak and Curly whimper inside the shirt-turned-knapsack twined across Yuki's shoulders. But

Sakurako didn't hesitate as she chose turn after turn in a winding, twisting labyrinth that led us who knew where.

Then the cold air outside descended into eerie silence, nothing but our own pants of exertion evident as moment after moment flowed past without any additional werewolf howls. We'd lost them, had shed our followers like winter fur wafted away by a breeze in springtime. And in that elation of survival, my pack bond momentarily flickered back to life....

Gunner, living. His lungs billowing and his muscles aching so drastically I stumbled over my next footstep.

Pain was acceptable, however. Pain and the knowledge that even though Gunner was losing the battle, I could now tell him that he'd won the war.

"We're safe," I attempted to shout down the pack bond. *"Stop fighting. Save yourself!"*

But my presence just spurred Gunner to work harder, leaping at his enemy until they went down together in a pile of fur and claws. Something broke in one of his extremities, something tore above his ribcage....

Then I was knocked backwards into my own body by brilliant lights above us combined with wind roaring so loudly it couldn't have been a natural part of the storm.

Sakurako squeezed out through a gap in the shrubbery, led us into a whirlwind of snow and ice. Above our heads, a helicopter hovered. Somehow, my grandmother had called upon human technology to complete our escape.

As I stared, a rope ladder fell from the open access hatch. The first of Sakurako's guards was already climbing up while the second reached down to grasp Kira's fox body in his arms.

This was it—the moment of decision. I could trust my grandmother to protect those I cared about and run back to assist my partner. Or I could follow her into the chopper and leave Gunner behind.

A mate wouldn't have hesitated, but I stood so long in the snow that ice formed pellets between my vulpine foot pads. Meanwhile, the fifth male knelt beside me, offering his arms as an easy route up.

This was the same male who'd sprayed our footprints as we entered the tunnel, the same one who might have tried to kill Gunner and actually killed Edward. Could I really leave him alone with my sister and a defenseless bloodling puppy? Could I trust any of these strangers to do the job I'd accepted as my own?

I couldn't and I didn't. But I did accept the male's offer of assistance, leaping into his arms and closing my eyes against the pain in my temples as he clambered upward into the aircraft above our heads.

Then we weren't hovering but rather flying. And my connection to Gunner abruptly winked all the way out.

Chapter 28

The pilot and I were the only ones awake by the time we landed, swooping in on a helipad on the roof of a mansion that made Gunner's city abode look like a run-down row house by comparison. Snow gusted away from the raised surface as we descended, but it was only a dusting. As if the vast blanket that had hindered our footsteps during our rush away from clan central had avoided this location...or as if Sakurako had another dozen minions on call just to sweep her roof clear.

The latter appeared to be the truth of the matter, because two additional specimens of perfect manhood came out to greet us as the helicopter rotors slowed from a roaring storm into a gentle breeze. The pair didn't even glance in my direction as they assisted Sakurako in descending, the robe that had been waiting for her in the chopper sweeping out behind them all like a bride's train.

Kira followed, eyes wide as she took in the lighted facade of the building, heated fountains flowing through zones of red and blue amid the snow below. "Wow," she breathed, spinning a circle so her own robe floated around her like a princess's, a few final snowflakes landing jewel-like in her hair.

Which meant I was the only one estimating the width of the windows while stiffly unfolding myself from the position in which I'd waited out the journey. How deep was the snow?

How far away was the road? Would the wrought-iron fence surrounding this residence keep enemy werewolves at bay?

"Three miles." Yuki's voice drew me out of the helicopter before Kira could follow our grandmother inside the mansion. His hand was strong as he helped me down onto the helipad, and I appreciated the support after a day that still stretched before me with no obvious conclusion in sight.

"Three miles?" I repeated, trying to make sense of the observation as I released his hand a little more quickly than I'd intended to. The memory of Gunner's pain made it difficult to touch another man.

"Three miles to the nearest roadway, and even that is gated and completely covered with snow at the moment. We're safe here, Mai-san. But you can bunk with me if it will help you sleep soundly tonight."

I glanced backwards at Yuki rather than taking in the opulence as we passed through the doorway, me leading and him hovering not far behind. If he was insinuating what I thought he was insinuating, perhaps Soba's attendants weren't my cousins after all....

We trailed the rest of the party down a circular staircase in the center of a tremendous, four-story atrium. There was more to look at here than there had been outside the residence, chandeliers and vast, shiny tables and vases large enough I could have stepped inside. Still, my attention was riveted on Yuki, trying to figure out how to reject his offer without coming across as irredeemably rude.

"Prepare our guests a chamber." My grandmother was the one who saved me from answering, sending Yuki away on an errand that even I knew had already been completed. He didn't complain, though. Merely bowed and left us even as Sakurako pulled me into a corner where I could keep an eye on Kira without worrying that anyone might overhear our words.

"Sobo, thank you for your hospitality," I started. But the high-handed kitsune shushed me in her usual manner, speaking over me without waiting for a lull.

"It's best not to play favorites, granddaughter. At least in the beginning. Later, once they all have a chance of being the father, it's easier to keep them at heel."

A chance of being the *father?* I must have twitched because Sakurako sighed, and for the first time looked the tiniest bit tired. "Sleep with Kira tonight if you're cold. That's all I ask from you."

That suggestion, at least, I could comply with. Well, except for the sleeping part. Because after Kira and Curly snuggled up together on the tremendous, canopied bed in their fur forms, I used the last gasp of my energy to materialize my star ball into its familiar sword shape. Then I sank down to the floor to listen for intruders while staring at Curly's side as it rose and fell with his breath.

He was just as cute as ever, but all I saw was a potential source of blood. Because the last of Edward's fluids had been lost on snowy leaf litter, so this tiny werewolf was my only remaining avenue to discover whether my partner had survived his ill-matched fight.

But I wasn't about to steal energy from a toddler, no matter whether both he and his mother had given overt approval of that course of action. So, laying my sword across my lap, I settled in to wait.

I MUST HAVE ENDED UP sleeping after all. Because when I woke, it was to Sakurako's crinkled fingers shaking me back to life.

"Granddaughter, walk with me."

Sunlight streamed through the windows so brilliantly I was pretty sure it was once again closer to lunch than to breakfast. And I considered waking Kira and Curly so I wouldn't have to let them out of my sight.

But Sakurako raised one eyebrow, reminding me of her promise. And I reluctantly admitted that her kitsune nature would force her to stick to her word.

So I nodded, following Sakurako past two males guarding the outside of my doorway. Then we traveled at a pace that should have been beyond such an elderly lady as we strode rapidly down the hall.

At first, I thought this was going to be another information-gathering session where my grandmother's stubbornness exceeded my ability to batter through it. But she only waited until we were beyond the range of Kira's hearing before she began filling me in.

"This is one of several properties our lineage manages," Sakurako told me, waving her hand at the expanse of snow-covered forest we could see through the long line of windows we were currently walking past. "There are four lineages left, ten kitsunes in the entire world that we know of." She paused, corrected herself. "No. With you and your sister, that total comes to twelve."

So few. The weight in my stomach was nothing compared to what settled there when I thought of Gunner—of Gunner who *had* to have survived the previous night. Still, it was significant that Kira and I each made up eight percent of the total world kitsune population. And it also explained the males who fawned over Sakurako...and the one who had already started fawning over me.

"That's why you wanted us to join you," I suggested. "To carry on that lineage. With, what, a harem of males to ensure we reproduce in a timely manner?"

"We call them an honor guard. They are chosen as much for their skills as for their genetics. But, yes, your statement is correct factually. The important point, however...."

I wasn't fated to learn what the important point was, unfortunately. Because Sakurako stepped closer to the glass expanse rather than finishing her explanation. And when I leaned sideways to see around her, my attention was captivated just as hers had been.

Outside, the snow was waist high with no plowed pathway to enable a vehicle to drive through it. According to Yuki, the road lay three miles distant with a gate blocking the way. And yet, a gray animal bounded through the drifts toward us, tail and ears iced over but the beast most definitively a wolf.

Chapter 29

"That's Elle." My first burst of fear was replaced by breathless anticipation as I discerned the werewolf's identity. Maybe my former mentor knew what had happened to Gunner. Maybe she'd come to inform me that her half-brother was safe.

But Sakurako was no longer close enough to hear my explanation. Instead, she'd pushed open the nearest window...and was now striding down a staircase of snow that I was 99% positive hadn't existed one moment before.

Meanwhile, wind created a mini spiral of white with my grandmother at its center. Her feet slid rather than stepped forward, skimming across the tops of drifts as if she was surfing. So this is what a kitsune could do at the height of her power. The snowstorm hadn't been a coincidence...and I hadn't even seen my grandmother charge herself up with werewolf blood.

I shivered in place for one split second, then I pushed through heavy snow in Sakurako's wake. Unlike my grandmother, I wasn't able to levitate so I had no chance of closing the distance between us. Still, Sakurako was slowed by the wrought-iron fence encircling her residence, and I nearly caught up as she melted drifted snow away from the gate.

I wasn't close enough to interrupt, however, as my grandmother spoke without a single glance in my direction. "You dare to invade my home without permission, werewolf?" Saku-rako's words didn't soften even as Elle struggled to regain her human form.

"I...used...the pack bond...to find...Mai...so I could deliver...a message. I came..." Gunner's half-sister looked pitiful, naked in the snow. Meanwhile, cold made her teeth chatter so rapidly she barely managed to spit out her words.

But I understood what she was saying. Understood that my connection to Elle was still strong enough to be used to locate me...which made the absence of a tether between myself and Gunner more ominous yet.

"Is...?" I started, not able to voice the possibility. In answer, Elle raised one hand to a strange, bulky choker encircling her neck.

And maybe my grandmother thought the choker was a weapon. Or maybe she was simply annoyed by the fact that Elle wasn't lying prostrate, groveling in the snow. Whatever the reason, a flash of light leapt between them, Elle flinched, then a long line of blood rose along the outside of my friend's arm.

"Sobo!" I yelled, as I attempted to push my way between them. "Elle is my friend! She isn't an invader! Leave her alone!"

Rather than answering, Sakurako reached toward the naked werewolf with bony, cronish fingers. Scooping up a streak of red, she brought it to her mouth. "Now she'll be obedient," the old woman agreed, turning at last to face me with the tiniest smear of blood clinging to one corner of her mouth.

This was last summer all over again. A kitsune stealing werewolf power to force those I cared about to obey someone else's will. And regardless of the fact that I was a guest in Saku-

rako's mansion, that wasn't a fate I could allow to befall someone I called my friend.

So, without another word, I pushed myself between the
two females. And this time it was me who stole a long lick from
Elle's blood-streaked forearm, claiming Gunner's half-sister as
my own.

I EXPECTED ANGER, BUT Sakurako only smiled and
turned her back on us both to lead the way toward a wide-
open door on the ground-floor level. The old woman should
have been angry that I'd contradicted her, but I got the distinct
impression this was, instead, the first time I'd ever made her
proud.

Ignoring the fleeting thought that I'd played directly into
the old woman's hands, I wrapped my arms around Elle to
warm her while explaining what I'd done. "I had to break her
hold over you, but I won't coerce you," I promised...feeling
like a hypocrite as I latched onto the burst of werewolf power
flooding my body in an attempt to connect with my not-quite-
mate.

Gunner, where are you? I pushed outwards with all my
might, attempting to rebuild the connection I'd lost yesterday.
But either the few drops of blood I'd consumed were too mi-
nuscule to overcome such a vast distance or the alpha wasn't
alive to answer. Either way, no pack bond flared to life between
us, and an uncontrollable shiver racked my body from head to
toe.

Although she had just as much reason to lose herself to the
darkness as I did, Elle was the one who brought me back to re-

ality. She planted her bare feet and tugged at the choker rather than continuing to follow me toward the door.

Only it wasn't a choker. It was a hollow collar that clicked open to reveal a slightly damp sheet of paper. "From Ransom," Elle managed between chattering teeth.

Ransom, not Gunner. Shoulders slumping, I accepted the letter only because Elle was so adamant about it, then I did my best to usher the naked female a little faster through the snow. She was so cold now that her lips were blue and she'd actually stopped shivering. Even I knew that couldn't be good.

But Sakurako's underlings were prepared for every eventuality. Two ran out to meet us wielding a big, woolly blanket, and I wrapped Elle up even as I snapped out orders at the others waiting just inside the door.

"We need a hot bath and someone who knows how to treat hypothermia," I demanded, ignoring the fact that my grandmother had chosen these men to be part of my honor guard. Giving them commands felt like a first step down a slippery slope that ended in me owning their bodies and souls. Like stealing blood from Elle, the notion made me subtly sick.

But my friend needed medical attention and she needed it immediately. So, ignoring the frisson of discomfort in my stomach, I accepted the bows of Sakurako's attendants and the way they sprinted off to do as I'd asked.

Then both Elle and I were inside, walking down a hallway into a room that was blissfully warm and decked out like a small-scale clinic. "I have medic training," Yuki offered as he sorted through a doctor's bag on the table beside him. "If you'll ask the patient to sit, I'll see what I can do."

He was clearly wary of touching a wounded, unpredictable werewolf. And, for her part, Elle was becoming more agitated rather than less so as we walked through the clinic door.

At first, I thought the issue was being surrounded by a kitsune's loyal retainers. But then the female grabbed my arm with surprisingly strong fingers before bringing the nearly forgotten paper up from where it dangled at my side.

"Read this," she managed between teeth chattering so badly they nicked her tongue.

"If you'll sit down, I'll read it," I soothed her. And, thankfully, my friend finally accepted the chair one of Sakurako's honor guard had pulled out for her use.

Her gaze remained focused on me, however, and she ignored Yuki's questions and promptings to bend and wiggle various body parts. So, finally, I gave in, unfolded the paper, and began to read as a way of getting this medical exam back on track.

"I'm ready to call in my debt."

I hunched over in surprise at the pain in my middle. Because a tether had been created just like the one I'd been trying to resurrect moments earlier. Too bad this bond led to the elder Atwood brother rather than to the one I wanted to connect with the most.

Ransom was west of me, not north on his island the way he should have been. And the rest of the message confirmed that point by listing an address only a few miles from where I'd left Gunner to be pounded up by another wolf.

The note ended with no explanation, just further orders: *"Come as soon as you are able. I'll be waiting for you."*

Chapter 30

"**G**randdaughter, if you have a moment...."

I froze in the darkness, fingers on the tank of the snowmobile I'd found along with five others in the basement. The debt had spurred me into immediate action, and I'd rightly guessed that my grandmother wouldn't bury her mansion under three feet of snow if she didn't have ground transportation at the ready. What I hadn't guessed was that she'd be able to find me so quickly when I slipped my leash and began exploring the residence on my own.

"Yes, Sobo?" I backed away from the vehicle and into the light of the hallway, mind buzzing through possible explanations for lurking down here in the darkness. What could I possibly say I'd been looking for other than an easy way out of her clutches? Usually adept at making up stories, I was currently drawing a blank.

"There are things you need to know, granddaughter." Sakurako's eyes flicked behind me once, but she spoke as if my location wasn't suspiciously telling. Still, I sensed her restraint in the hum of kitsune power seething beneath her skin. The old woman was currently stronger than I'd ever seen her. As if summoning snowstorms revved her up rather than wearing her down.

And maybe Sakurako's skills included mind reading, because she went on to confirm my analysis of her strength. "You've been dabbling in the barest edges of kitsune power, granddaughter. Blood magic is minor and fleeting. I can show you how to harvest energy from the adoration of your honor guard and even from the sky."

There it was, out in the open. For days she'd been dancing around this subject and I was suddenly sick of fending off advances without knowing for sure what we were talking about.

So I stepped in a little closer, accepting the direct path. "Stop beating around the bush, Sakurako. What exactly do you want from me?"

My grandmother was small and alone there in the basement, with the brittle bones and sagging skin of old age. But her words were powerful as she told me: "I want you to live here, be my apprentice, accept your honor guard, and take over this lineage after I'm gone."

For the last few days, some rainbows-and-kittens part of me had insisted I'd be able to maintain a relationship with my grandmother without falling into her world completely. But there was too much at stake now to dream of impossibilities. So I countered: "If I won't?"

"If you won't, then I'll be forced to select another heiress."

Well, that didn't sound so bad. Money and properties were irrelevant. For the first time all day, my shoulders relaxed away from my ears...too soon, as I discovered when my grandmother continued to speak.

"I've been the epitome of patience, granddaughter. But the time has come for you to make a choice. Do you want to be my apprentice, or would you rather I trained your sister instead?"

"WHAT HAVE YOU DONE with Kira?" Despite the fact that weapons were of little use against magic, my sword was at the old woman's throat as soon as she'd spoken.

Unfortunately, Sakurako reacted just as quickly. She twitched her fingers ever so slightly...then my sword began dissolving into pure magic that seeped like lotion into her skin.

Yelping, I yanked back all that remained to me, hiding my star ball inside my body where it couldn't be stolen. But I'd lost a third of my energy already, the absence making my legs shake so badly they threatened to drop me onto my face.

Sakurako wasn't just powerful...she was unbeatable. A supervillain laughing at the weakness of mere mortals as she soared above us with cape streaming in the wind.

Still, I stood up to the old woman, measuring the distance between us carefully. She was, when it came right down to it, small and relatively feeble. It was possible I could overpower her with my bare hands alone....

"Kira is perfectly safe," Sakurako answered before I'd decided whether it was worth trying to strangle one of my two remaining relatives in order to save the other one. "And she will remain safe, along with your pet werewolves, while you prove your worth and goodwill. Now come."

Without waiting for an answer, she turned her back on me and began striding toward the staircase that led back to the living area above us. And I had no choice but to trot after her, realizing as I did so that yesterday's twenty-four-hour oath must have recently lapsed.

That explained why the kid gloves had come off my grandmother. But it also gave me an inkling of a solution....

Unfortunately, Ransom's debt still tugged at my stomach, making it difficult to ascend behind Sakurako rather than returning to the basement and leaving this mansion behind me. Only the fact that I didn't actually know how to drive a snowmobile prevented the Atwood werewolf's demand from determining my immediate future.

So...maybe if I could pin my grandmother down to a similar promise, I could ensure my friends didn't suffer for my mistakes. Of course, I'd have to give something to get something. Good thing I had a bargaining chip on hand.

"Oyo." The name of the black-furred fox Sakurako had demanded I hand over made the old woman pause. She turned to face me from two steps higher, leaving us standing eye to eye.

"You say her name as if you know her." So my grandmother had only been guessing earlier when she'd asked for the black fox who'd showed up terrified at my party. Well, I was only guessing now as I pieced together information that would allow me to break my oath to someone I'd promised to protect.

"She was your original heir, wasn't she?" I ascended one step until I was even closer to my grandmother, looking down now in order to meet her eyes. "You trained her to use affection to harvest magic. Then, what, you heard about me and Kira and you tossed her aside?"

"I didn't *toss* anyone. The ungrateful wench left me."

"Left you and followed the breadcrumbs you'd uncovered to Atwood clan central. No wonder my pack started to crumble as soon as she arrived."

Because Gunner was an excellent alpha. He would never have let so many resentments smolder beneath the surface, just waiting to flare up into fur-form fights.

No, it was Oyo's presence that had been the instigating factor. Her presence...and maybe magic she'd used on the sly?

Either way, I could feel my promise to the black-furred kitsune sloughing off as I prepared to make Sakurako an offer I hoped she couldn't refuse. I'd need proof that my guesses held water, but if Oyo was the one responsible for killing Edward....

"I'll bring you Oyo. You can breed her to your harem, end up with two young kitsunes to raise as you wish." The offer was horrendous—I was signing Oyo's death warrant and setting up her children for a lifetime of servitude...the same sort of servitude I would also be forced to accept.

"Along with Oyo, I'll obey you, do whatever you ask of me...." I swallowed, hating the fact that my voice cracked as I sealed my fate.

"And in exchange, granddaughter?"

"In exchange, you'll relinquish Kira, Elle, and Curly. You'll return them to their home and never contact them or any other werewolves ever again."

Chapter 31

With Sakurako as an ally, transport to Ransom's proposed meeting location was simple and expedient. I boarded the helicopter beside Yuki, Elle, and Curly, reluctantly leaving my sister behind after a brief bear hug.

"Be strong. I'll come back for you tomorrow," I whispered into the top of her head...which was now closer to my nose than to my chin. In the midst of all the drama, my sister was growing. And her answer proved that point.

"*You* be strong," countered my little sister. "Don't worry about me. I'll be fine."

Which left me with only one final family member to speak with before I climbed into the aircraft slated to carry me away for a very short while. "You promised another twenty-four hours of leeway," I hissed at my grandmother. "I expect you to leave Kira alone while you wait."

We'd already hashed this out an hour earlier and I *thought* I'd trapped the wily old kitsune into a binding oath. Well, I *hoped* I'd trapped her. But it still felt like driving on the left side of the road to leave my sister behind for even a single day.

"You do your job and I'll do my job," Sakurako answered, which wasn't as heartening as she might have supposed.

Or maybe she knew her words weren't heartening. Perhaps this was just another test to determine whether I was worth cultivating in Kira's place.

So I stiffened my spine and stooped to rush under the blades of the helicopter, which were already spinning their way up to gale-force speed. I'd neutralize Oyo, relieve my debt to Ransom, then return to take my place by my grandmother's side.

And Gunner? I squashed the thought as soon as it rose within me. This was why we'd never fully mated. Because my own wishes had to play second fiddle to the safety of those I cared about.

Elle raised her brows as I joined her, widened her eyes yet further when Yuki reached over to pull me onto his lap. The helicopter wasn't so small we needed to share seating, but I knew the hard decision Yuki would soon be faced with and didn't argue. Instead, I fingered the cold shard of magic in my pocket and watched Elle pet Curly, wondering whether I'd made the right choice by bringing the werewolf pup along.

Unfortunately, there was no safe place for a bloodling at present. Not when the youngster was too useful to Sakurako to leave behind and too distasteful to hidebound alphas to be integrated into Ransom's pack. Elle, however, I could depend upon to protect a bloodling puppy. Now that she'd regained her color and her energy, I trusted my not-quite-sister-in-law as much as I trusted Gunner to keep an eye out for the weak.

Gunner. Again, I pushed his face out of my mind. Refused to consider the fact that my partner might be dead already. Couldn't fathom the thought of leaving him forever if he still lived.

So, instead, I watched the sunset as we flew westward, darkness descending over the half-melted snow beneath us. Was it only three nights since Kira and I had surreptitiously moved into our werewolf-scented cottage? Only seventy-two hours since I'd been hopeful about life as the mate of a werewolf pack leader with no notion of what my heritage meant for those caught in the crossfire?

Then the helicopter was hovering over an open field, a car waiting to carry us to the spot Ransom had designated for our meeting. I'd borrowed a cell phone and called ahead with our itinerary, but I still expected to be made to wait on the other end of our travels.

Only I wasn't. The instant we pulled up in front of the fast-food joint, Ransom rushed out to meet us. Despite tinted windows, he somehow chose the door closest to me and opened it with a hard yank. Then he drew me out of the vehicle so roughly I had to struggle against instinct, barely managing to keep my star ball under wraps.

Patience, I warned myself, crossing my arms to prevent my fists from striking my accoster. If I had any hope of convincing Ransom to save his brother rather than using me to depose Gunner, I had to keep my head.

Ransom, on the other hand, had descended into that werewolf ball of fury where he was physically human but emotionally a wolf. "I require you to fulfill your debt," he demanded, eyes blazing as he towered above me. And I knew I'd lost the gamble because I hadn't even been granted a single second in which to state my case.

"I'm ready." The words were yanked out of me by magic, my head bending down in submission despite every impulse to keep the angry werewolf in my sights. Had I misread the elder brother's character? Now, finally, was the moment of truth.

Or it would have been if Ransom hadn't started pacing a circle around me without speaking. Would have been if he hadn't waited until my knees were trembling and my breath gasping before he put me out of my misery at last.

"You will go into Atwood clan central, and you will save my brother from whatever danger he faces. *That* is what I require in exchange for your debt."

"SO HE'S ALIVE?" I GRABBED Ransom's arm as much to keep myself upright as to stop the relentless, circular pacing that was making my head whirl uncomfortably. In response, his brow furrowed exactly the way Gunner's did when he wasn't following the conversation, the similarity sucking away the remainder of my breath.

Unfortunately, Ransom's answer didn't help jumpstart my breathing. "I don't know. I expected you to know. Mate woo-woo and all that." He waved his hands around to indicate tether magic, and I suddenly wondered whether this so-called alpha had ever managed to see the connections within his own clan during the years he'd spent leading a pack.

So Ransom knew no more than I did. Gunner might be dead already. I closed my eyes for one split second then took a deep breath and returned to my original plan. Ransom had feet on the ground and a wish to help his brother. It was better to use him than to go off half-cocked without any information at all.

I opened my mouth to ask questions...just as Curly leapt through the open limousine door and into Ransom's arms. Despite myself, I laughed at the incongruous picture. This was exactly the way the puppy greeted Gunner. Too bad the elder Atwood brother was less amenable to the invasion of his space.

"You brought a *pet* to a war council?" I don't think he intended to punch Curly, but the hand intended to ward off the youngster's approach turned into a blow anyway. Yelping, Curly retreated beneath the vehicle, prompting Elle and Yuki to disembark and pull him out.

"And what is *that*?" Ransom continued, staring at the human while making the hair on the back of my neck stand on end with his use of "what" instead of "who." Dehumanizing much?

"That's an ally," I said simply. "Now tell me what you know about clan central."

And he did, finally, after Curly was stuffed back inside the limousine and Yuki was similarly out of sight beside Elle. It took the alpha half an hour to tell me, but what it boiled down to could be summed up in just a few key points.

The alphas and selected warriors from three neighboring packs had sealed the borders of Atwood clan central sometime late yesterday. Ransom had managed to send in multiple scouts, but none had reemerged.

What *had* come out was a message promising to cleanse the Atwood pack of dangerous kitsunes. "When they're done, they plan to divide the territory," Ransom finished, his feet once again carrying him in circles which I was now almost agitated enough to join him in.

"They plan to divide the territory," I repeated, not wanting to state the obvious—that if Atwood territory was about to be divvied up, that meant no alpha remained to head up Gunner's friends and family.

"Which is where you come in." Whatever his feelings about bloodlings, Ransom and I were of one mind when it came to Gunner. "They want a kitsune, we'll give them a kitsune. Then they'll let my brother free."

Chapter 32

The snow had turned crusty by the time Yuki and I strode into Atwood clan central an hour later. Ransom's intel suggested the village should have been full of all the werewolves I'd left behind plus a strong contingent of invading neighbors. But the streets were empty, porch lights were extinguished, and the entire area was as silent as the grave.

It reeked of sulfur, however. The rotten-egg aroma nipped at my nostrils from the first moment I stepped out of the limousine and it grew stronger and stronger as I followed pack bonds illuminated by Elle's freely offered blood.

Both sulfur stench and pack bonds led me in the same direction. The community hall. It rose before us, tall and looming...and loud with raised voices apparently engaged in extended debate.

"...has not yet been decided!" This was a stranger, no one I recognized. But from the timbre of his voice, I suspected he might be Gunner's counterpart from one of the neighboring territories.

"Isn't it obvious, Russell? This pack has fallen under the sway of a kitsune. Without further information, the safest course of action is to slay them all."

The words should have been chilling. But, instead, it was all I could do not to dance and sing right there on the sidewalk.

Because I was close enough now to disentangle the ropes of light arrowing away from my midriff, and one in particular let me breathe fully for the first time in what felt like days.

Stroking the wide tether with one cautious finger, I could hardly believe this bond sprang out straight and true from my person. I couldn't still be connected to a dead werewolf, could I? If not...then this thick rope of light meant Gunner hadn't perished when I left him behind to be overwhelmed by a stronger wolf.

Whether Gunner's life continued after today, however, was apparently up to the neighboring alphas. So I was relieved when a third voice spoke up, calm and measured and apparently on my side.

"Easy for you to say when your clan has been at odds with the Atwoods for generations." So we had at least one supporter on this council. It was good to know...and that fact made it easier for me to walk on past the community hall's main entrance, nodding at Yuki to separate our paths as I continued following the evidence of my nose.

Because the sulfurous reek was strong around the front of the community hall...but it emanated from above rather than from within. Without the need for words, Yuki padded silently along a fire escape leading up the west face of the building while I mirrored his movements on the opposite side.

The climb was simple, even in human form. Near the top, however, I hesitated, letting Yuki draw ahead of me.

Because he was my ace in the hole and the solution to the dueling compulsions in my belly. So I hung back as my human bait stepped toward Oyo, giving him time to prepare the path so I could turn my former charge over to a fate worse than death.

THE WAIT WAS AGONIZING. So I occupied myself peering through a dirty clerestory window into the meeting space below me.

Gunner. He was the first thing I saw, and for long seconds the only thing I had eyes for. My never-to-be mate was bound and gagged atop a raised dais, naked save for the ropes that encircled both body and chair in a complicated arrangement I assumed was meant to contain him even if he attempted to shift.

Gunner's attention, however, wasn't on me, or even on the alpha werewolves arguing beside him. Instead, his gaze was trained upon Atwood pack members huddled together in the main section of the hall.

Or, rather, upon the males and children huddling while females stood around them with weapons at the ready. The guards included Elizabeth, Becky, plus several other shifters I'd met in passing. They weren't protecting their clan mates, however. Instead, the females were preventing rebellion as ably as Gunner's ropes and gag currently restrained him.

Had the Atwood females gotten so angry with the pack's misogyny that they'd risen up against their mates, fathers, and brothers? Or was this just another indication that Oyo's powers were far greater than I'd originally supposed?

"Oyo-chan."

Yuki's murmured endearment drew my attention away from the odd disloyalty of the Atwood females...but not before I saw them react to a word they shouldn't have been able to hear. Elizabeth, in particular, nearly swiped her sword across a neighbor's belly as she raised one arm as if to soothe an aching forehead. Beside her, Becky—who I'd never seen wield a sword before—winced and sliced apart the top of her boot.

So Oyo *was* manipulating my pack mates just as I'd suspected. Was manipulating them...and had almost lost her hold in surprise at being discovered by the male she'd once considered more than a pawn.

This was evidence enough for me...but apparently not sufficient to relieve my magically fueled debt to Oyo. Because my feet still refused to move as I fingered the shard of magic Sakurako had provided. Instead, I waited as the other kitsune spoke.

"You came for me," the female whispered. And from the rustle of movement on the rooftop, I suspected she and Yuki were engaging in a hasty embrace of greeting.

"I will always come for you, Oyo-chan," he assured her. "But I knew you were clever enough to hold your own."

"Clever." Her laugh was a fox's bark, short and almost painful. "Was it clever to kill that werewolf? Edmund? Edward? Whatever. I thought he was Mai's enemy, but his death only made matters worse. And now look what's happening...."

There. That was the admission I'd been waiting for, the confirmation that Oyo had been poaching on my pack bonds, using my debt to manipulate those who cared about me.

And yet...I remained crouched on the snowy fire escape with head bowed, trying to think of another solution. Trying to think of a way out that didn't involve turning Oyo over to Sakurako to mate herself to death.

Because, yes, the black-furred fox was both a manipulator and a murderer. But she'd also been raised as the pawn of my grandmother, trained to fixate the attention of a harem of human males in an effort to steal their power. In her shoes would I have been any more ethical? Would I have been any less desperate to escape?

But there was no other solution available to me. My hard-earned protection for Kira was ticking away by the second. Meanwhile, beneath us, the neighboring alphas converged upon Gunner, the same enforcer who had beaten my partner now slicing through his gag carelessly enough to leave a line of red running down Gunner's cheek.

"Explain again why you believe this pack is salvageable." This was the voice of the Atwood-friendly alpha, but from above I could see how tired even our supposed ally was growing of the debate.

"My mate is a kitsune." Gunner's voice was hoarse and scratchy, as if he'd said the same thing half a dozen times previously. "She is not responsible for this problem. If you'll let her return, she'll stop the problem in its tracks."

"Or cover it up." This was the alpha most obviously against us, and beside him the third pack leader nodded his head in agreement. No, I couldn't trust these werewolves to come to the appropriate decision and save Gunner.

So, without allowing myself to think about what I was doing, I hopped onto the rooftop, strode fox-silent up behind Oyo, and slapped the frigid shard of magic into Yuki's waiting hand.

Chapter 33

Oyo was deeply entwined in the arms of her lover, but my grandmother had been right—she sensed the shard of magic the instant it touched him. Struggling to free herself, her eyes met mine for a split second...just as Yuki thrust the magical dagger directly into his beloved's breast.

I'd thought I was prepared for this eventuality. After all, Sakurako had assured me this was only a magical neutering, not a death blow. But I still flinched at the horror on Oyo's face as she realized that the man she loved had conspired with the woman she'd trusted in order to take her down.

Light flared around her body as fox ears sprouted from the top of a still-human forehead. The sulfurous stench deepened as Oyo cringed down over her belly, moaning as she was caught in the worst sort of shift.

"I thought you loved me," she cried...or at least I guessed that was what she was saying. Because vulpine teeth were now sprouting past lips that had been plump and human a moment earlier. Her words were almost irreparably slurred.

Then Oyo could speak no longer. The flare of light shrouded her, shrunk her...and settled into a golden collar encircling the throat of a black-furred fox. At the same time, the rotten-egg aroma was abruptly and entirely gone.

Beneath us, the meeting erupted into shouting followed by the unmistakable metallic clangs of swordplay. Oyo's hold over my pack mates had faded the instant she was separated from her powers and I *needed* to get below as quickly as possible to make sure neighbor werewolves didn't do anything terrible in their haste to regain the upper hand.

But, instead, I stood frozen by the tableau before me. Watched and listened as Yuki proved that Oyo wasn't the only one who had been broken by my grandmother's heavy-handed control.

"I love the mistress," Yuki answered coldly. "And I loved you when I thought you might one day be the new mistress. Unfortunately, it looks like that will no longer be the case."

Then he turned away as if Oyo was nothing, never mind the fact that the fox he ignored was scratching so frantically at her collar that it spun around and around her throat without stopping. In half an hour, she'd be raw and bleeding. But Sakurako had assured me Oyo would never get the restraining circlet off.

And, given the certainty of his job's completion, Yuki simply didn't care about the agony he had left behind. Didn't even reach out to calm Oyo's scratching to prevent future pain to the shifter he supposedly cared for. Instead, he strode over to the fire escape, preparing to guard my pathway to the ground.

This was the pack I was willingly walking into. This was the pack I'd chosen as my own.

For Kira's sake, I reminded myself. Then ignoring my own squeamishness, I snapped a lead onto Oyo's collar. "Let's go," I told her as I followed the male down.

BY THE TIME WE REACHED the door at the front of the community hall, the interior had become a battleground with no clear evidence of who might win. Atwoods outnumbered the invaders by a wide margin, but only the sword-bearing females seemed willing to do more than protect themselves.

Instead, it was as if the command Gunner uttered three days earlier—fight only with swords—had gone into effect with a belated vengeance. Which gave our enemies an extreme advantage as they pressed in against the ring of females now intent upon safeguarding rather than containing their family and friends.

"Where to?" Yuki asked, his sword angling across to guard me rather than his own body. Together, we watched wolves in their prime lunge at Atwood grannies while Gunner's best warriors snapped, feinted...then failed to fight back.

This was going to be a slaughter if we didn't shut it down quickly. So despite Yuki's not-so-subtle wish for us to return to Sakurako's secluded hideout, I told him the obvious: "I'm going to cut off the head of the serpent." In other words, I intended to make the invading alphas call off their underlings by hook or by crook.

And, to my surprise, Yuki didn't even attempt to argue. "Sounds like fun," he admitted. Then, glancing at Oyo and raising his eyebrows, he added: "May I?"

It seemed cruel to place the collared fox into the arms of her former lover. But I wasn't used to fighting with a living being tucked under one arm and I *needed* to reach Gunner ASAP. So I nodded...then lost track of Yuki entirely as I took a running leap onto the top of a banister that encircled one side of the room.

From my elevated perch, I could see the invaders much better....and, unfortunately, could be seen by them as well. So I wasn't surprised to be met by a wall of weapons at the far end of my raised pathway, proving that the Atwood tradition of swordcraft extended to the neighboring packs.

"I don't suppose you guys would like to let me through to talk to your alphas?" I called downward...then dove forward without waiting for a reply. Because at any minute the enemy alphas would realize they only had to threaten Gunner in order to make his entire pack—including me—submit to the boot poised atop our neck.

Which would leave us in a worse bind than we currently suffered from. So I slashed and parried and noted that the five males I faced were good enough to overcome a lone swordswoman of any caliber if given enough time. Which meant I couldn't risk disarming them gradually. I'd have to dole out more punishing blows and hope the injuries didn't scuttle future reconciliation with neighboring packs.

Or that would have been the case if two warm bodies hadn't materialized at my shoulders. Elizabeth on one side, the male who'd snarled during our sword practice on the other. Neither one had a reason to help me, and Elizabeth had a very good reason to push me in front of a bus.

After all, even though I hadn't wanted anything to happen to her father, I had indeed turned out to be the reason for his death. But perhaps Elizabeth hadn't yet come to that conclusion. Or perhaps pack was simply more important to her than personal grudges. Whatever the reason, she met my gaze evenly before she and her companion both dove into the battle so furiously I was able to slip around my opponents and ascend the stairs onto the stage.

"You came back."

The enforcer who'd beaten Gunner stood before me, and I barely managed not to skewer him in retaliation for the pain he'd doled out. But this battle wouldn't be won with a weapon. Instead, I let my sword trickle back into my skin while I peered over the enforcer's shoulder and met the eyes of three neighboring alphas one by one.

The males were glancing back and forth between me and Yuki, who held Oyo in his arms in a very visible spot at the other end of the hall. The visual aid was appreciated, so I used it. "I've collared the rogue kitsune," I told the alphas, having to raise my voice almost into a shout to be heard above the battle. "Her power has been neutralized and she will be punished...."

I'd intended to continue explaining then to move on to threats if necessary, stopping only when the neighboring alphas released their hold over all Atwood wolves. But to my surprise, Gunner was the one who answered, his voice rough, urgent, yet entirely clear.

"No, Mai, you can't do that. Oyo is under my protection. I refuse to allow you to trade her life for mine."

Chapter 34

"**G**unner, you have to trust me."

This wasn't the time to explain the full extent of Oyo's awfulness. I couldn't mention my grandmother's magic in front of the assembled alphas either, not if the goal was to assure our opponents that the Atwood pack was no longer under a kitsune's sway.

Especially since I could already see the three strange alphas turning against me. "This is your mate?" asked the fence-sitter, his face not giving away a single clue about whether my sword-wielding appearance had swayed him over to the other side of the fence.

"Yes." Gunner was firm, but his brow remained furrowed. Meanwhile, he neglected to back up my assertion that Oyo had been the one responsible for manipulating his clan.

"And you believe she's truly partnering with you rather than controlling you?" This was the neighbor whose apparent goal was to behead Gunner and take over at least a portion of his territory. "Then you should have regained control of your pack by now. Tell them to stop fighting..."

"...And you'll do the same for your wolves?" Gunner wasn't an idiot so he didn't trust the greedy alpha as far as he could throw him. Still, his attention remained riveted on me rather than on his opponent, sienna eyes searching my face.

Gunner was buying time while coming to a decision, I realized. So I pushed as hard as I could to send information down our tether the way he'd once shared his own vision. If Gunner heard Oyo's admission in my memory, then he'd stop looking for another solution that didn't involve the redhead being punished for her past actions....

But the tether—still obvious and visible with Elle's blood empowering me—remained inert beneath my hand. And, finally, Gunner came to a decision without any additional information. "I'll..." he started, only to be interrupted by a change in the sounds of battle echoing up to us from the floor of the hall.

At first, I thought that the conflict between Atwoods and invaders had been settled. Why else would a lull be rolling across the crowd? Then I noted that the Atwood sword-wielders were still fighting frantically. It was their opponents who turned in a wave to face the doorway that I had recently come through.

And no wonder when that dark rectangle was no longer empty and open to the snowy night beyond it. Instead, Ransom stood bold and tall in its center, innumerable well-armed shifters at his flank.

Backup had arrived. Backup...or a deposed alpha ready to take his rightful place at the head of the clan he'd been ejected from. I shivered, hesitated. Gunner, in contrast, trusted his sibling implicitly.

"Stand down," he commanded his underlings. And as the wave of discarded weapons fell from the hands of my students, Ransom's pack mates raised their own blades to take over the fight.

Gunner had proven his control without giving our enemies the advantage. And Ransom had been the ally who made that parry work.

"I'LL BE WATCHING YOU."

The least friendly neighboring alpha stepped past us as I slipped my sword through Gunner's bonds to free him. And even though he should have been stiff and sore after hours without moving, Gunner rose as lithely as he'd leapt from the trunk of Old Red two days before.

"The feeling is mutual," my partner growled as I stepped around the pair of them to deal with my own problems. Where was she? In the midst of the Atwood reunion and enemy out-flux, it took a long moment to find the black-furred fox within the crowd.

But there was Yuki holding tightly onto Oyo. I'd been half fearful that Kira's ticket to safety would have escaped while my attention was elsewhere, or that Yuki would have changed his mind again, taken his lover, and run. But the duo instead waited just past the edges of the fighting...beneath a clock that promised I had only nineteen hours left before my sister's safety ran thin.

Nineteen hours and a ten-hour drive to fit into that window. Because the helicopter had departed immediately after dropping us off. Which left me so little time to spend with my never-to-be partner before leaving his pack behind for good....

I turned back around just as the third and final alpha spoke to Gunner. "Our agreement still stands?" This was the pro-Atwood neighbor nailing down details of yet another alliance.

Gunner clearly wasn't done saying farewell to his uninvited house guests, so this time I turned my attention to Elle instead.

"Can you watch them for me?" I mouthed, silently tugging on our tether to get her attention before cutting my eyes to Yuki and Oyo. I didn't expect my friend to hear me, but comprehension dawned on her face more easily than it should have. Was this what it would have been like to be part of a pack?

Sure enough, Elle was already pushing through the crowd toward Yuki and Oyo even though her mouth was now pinched into a straight line. She disagreed with my intention to turn myself back over to Sakurako. But apparently she was willing to assist me in the matter nonetheless.

Then the community hall was emptying, enemy shifters leaving as quickly as they'd come. Meanwhile, wolves from both Atwood packs intermingled, spending a few precious minutes with one-time neighbors they hadn't seen for several months due to the actions of their alphas.

Which left Gunner and Ransom alone on the dais...well, alone except for me.

"Brother." Gunner held out one hand to his sibling, waiting a beat longer than I would have for reciprocation that clearly wasn't forthcoming before allowing the appendage in question to drop back down to his side. Still, he continued attempting to build bridges. "I'm glad you've come home. It's high time we learned to rule together."

Together. It was a tremendous admission...but apparently not quite tremendous enough to mollify the older brother. Because Ransom remained dour as he eyed Gunner consideringly. Then, slowly, he shook his head.

"I will be your ally if you support my bid for the northern territory," Ransom growled. "But don't think I'm going to retreat with my tail between my legs to accept your scraps. You cast us out and we've made new lives for ourselves. Lives that don't involve bloodlings and kitsunes and losing ground our grandfather bought."

Beneath us, the members of both Atwood packs let their conversations falter into silence, shifter ears catching every word from up above. This wasn't the reconciliation Gunner had been hoping for...but at least it wasn't the coup I'd feared.

"Take what Ransom offers," I begged Gunner silently, wishing once again that he could hear my words.

And maybe he did. Because my never-mate's eyes slipped toward me momentarily, then he nodded graciously. "Of course I'll support your territory, brother. I hope the lines of communication will remain open between our packs."

Chapter 35

A t long last, Ransom was gone, Gunner's underlings had settled in for the night, and I was alone with my never-to-be mate. Without Kira present to necessitate the keeping up of appearances, he drew me not toward my cottage but toward his own residence...a home that was considerably larger than it had been the last time I'd walked through its doors.

"This is Kira's room," I guessed, turning an awestruck circle within the addition that Gunner had created on the far side of his living room. There were fox ledges on the walls for playing in fur form, a glass-fronted cabinet full of yearned-for magic-trick paraphernalia, a full-size desk for schoolwork, and of course the mandatory canopied princess bed.

"Mm hm," Gunner answered, hovering so close to my body I could feel his heat without our skin ever touching. The alpha's restraint was doing crazy things to my thermal-regulation system...and his subsequent words were like a bucket of cold water poured over my head. "Where is my favorite teenager anyway?"

This was the beginning of the questions I couldn't answer...well, that I couldn't answer without losing the few hours I'd hoped to spend in Gunner's arms. So, rather than lying to a wolf who could detect prevarication through pure instinct, I curled my finger through his belt loop and drew him away from the teenager's paradise and toward the adult bedroom at the other end of his home.

"Come to bed," I murmured, plucking at his sleeve as he hesitated in the doorway then recoiling as my finger slipped across an open wound and came away bloody. His current pain was my fault...and I'd just made it even worse.

To my surprise, Gunner didn't wince at being poked in the middle of a red and angry laceration. Instead, he chuckled, grabbing my hand and replacing it around his wrist.

"I'm not so broken I can't welcome you home properly," he told me, using one hand to fumble at buttons that nonetheless obeyed his command with alacrity.

It was finally happening, the moment I'd been craving for weeks. So why did my heart hurt when Gunner paused before continuing, speaking a sentiment we hadn't yet shared aloud?

"I love you."

Three words. Three arrows piercing lungs and stomach and head as certainly as if they'd been made of wood and steel and murderous intention. I froze, unable to answer as the reality of my choice became thoroughly clear.

Because this was what I'd be losing when I returned to my grandmother tomorrow. Sure, Sakurako was an old woman. Eventually, she'd die and leave me to make my own choices. But even though becoming her apprentice wasn't a life sentence, I'd never again be someone Gunner looked at so warmly. Not after being molded by my grandmother's iron will.

I couldn't bear the thought of the alpha's disappointment upon seeing what I was fated to turn into. And I couldn't risk harming pack mates who had already lost so much at a kitsune's hand.

So once I left this home, I'd never again see Atwood clan central. Instead, I'd trust the alpha who might have been my mate to raise my sister. And I'd treat his memory as a spark of fire to warm an increasingly frigid heart.

Eventually, I'd be just like my grandmother. Eventually I'd stop caring. If I was lucky, I might even begin to forget.

My face must have broadcast this tumult of emotions because Gunner's caresses turned platonic and soothing, his huge hand cupping my chin. "I don't expect an answer," he told me, incorrectly interpreting my lack of a reply as a continuation of my ongoing independence battle. "I'm just happy to have you beside me. I'm so grateful that you're here."

And I *was* here. For an hour or two—the most I could spare from Sakurako's timeline. I shivered as the full force of the future brushed up against me. And Gunner, always attuned to my emotions, provided yet another opening for me to get weighty secrets off my chest.

"Do you want to talk about it?"

Gunner was willing to ignore the demands of our flesh and hash out the argument that still simmered unresolved between us. But I wasn't. Not when any explanation would leave me without the single memory I ached to carry with me back into the snow.

"Tomorrow," I answered, brushing my lips against Gunner's. But those final words were a lie, because in the morning I intended to be gone.

I WOKE IN GUNNER'S arms an uncountable number of hours later, my heart pounding with fear that I'd overslept. I hadn't meant to close my eyes at all, actually. Had intended to wait out Gunner's exhaustion then leave once he was deeply asleep.

Only, I'd been the one to wear myself out and descend into slumber. I'd been the one to snuggle into his safe harbor and forget about the impending storm.

Now, as I gently disentangled myself from the werewolf I'd once thought would be my life partner, I powered up my cell phone and sent Elle the long-awaited text. *"Bring Yuki and Oyo. We're going."*

"Are you sure?" she countered immediately, clearly wide awake and waiting for me.

"Be ready in five minutes," was my only answer. Of course I wasn't sure...but I'd do whatever had to be done.

It wasn't as late as I'd thought, however. So I slipped into the kitchen, found a pen and pad of paper, and sat down to explain myself to the mate I was leaving behind.

Because it wasn't fair to leave Gunner dangling. Wasn't fair to make him think I was rejecting our mating through anything other than a desperate bid to save my sister's last few years of childhood. The only way to even the scales a smidgeon was to tell the truth so he could find another female to fill the hole in his pack and his heart.

"I need to explain," I started. Scratched that out and tried another opening: *"It isn't because of you that I'm doing this...."*

Okay, that was so trite as to be depressing. Gunner deserved to understand how I really felt. And this time when I pushed my pen's point into the paper, the words finally began to flow.

"I have to leave for the sake of my sister," I started. *"But in my heart, you will always be my mate...."*

Only, rather than finishing my explanation, the pen streaked a crazy line across the paper. Then it fell out of nerveless fingers as our mate bond clicked into place with the force of a tractor trailer hitting a pedestrian on a crosswalk.

For an instant, my vision dimmed, my ears rang, and I lost all track of reality. "You implied I had to *say* the words," I moaned in protest.

Wait, had I sent that emoting down the mate bond? Had Gunner felt the contact even though he slept?

I gasped, trying to regain enough breath to rush out of the house without looking backwards. I couldn't afford to be bogged down in explanations with Kira's future on the line. Plus, if Gunner understood what I was planning, he'd never let me go....

But my legs crumpled beneath me and I ended up leaning against the counter instead of sprinting away out the door. All I could do was beg silently: *"Stay where you are. Stay safe,"* as wooden legs gradually carried me through the kitchen at the speed of a beer-soaked garden snail. One step after the other, from counter to counter to cabinet to door.

There. I was walking almost normally again even though the pain in my stomach was so intense I would have thrown up if I'd bothered eating before I slept. This I could handle. Being mated then leaving my mate forever wasn't so horrible....

And as if the thought had called agony back into existence, I doubled up over a spear of pain as intense as a sword slicing into my gut.

Gut wounds are usually fatal, I thought vaguely. Then, more clearly—*Ten hours is all I have left.*

I refused to leave Kira to our grandmother's mercy. So I straightened, looked down at a stomach I'd thought would be bleeding but wasn't. Finding no wound evident, I opened the door and walked out into the night.

Chapter 36

"This is a terrible idea," Elle informed me. "You can't even drive."

I leaned back against the heated, leather seat on the passenger side of the vehicle, trying to ignore how disloyal I felt taking the car Gunner had bought me while making my escape. Glancing back over my shoulder, I assured myself that Yuki and Oyo were sleeping. Then I countered, "I *can* drive. You just wouldn't let me behind the wheel."

"Because you look like death. You do realize Gunner will feel exactly like you do when he wakes up and finds you missing?"

No, I hadn't realized that. Somehow, I'd assumed the pain of mating then leaving would all be mine to bear. The knowledge that Gunner would deal with the same sort of agony started my head pounding as if Kira were using my skull as her own personal drum.

"Can I protect him by breaking the mate bond?" I didn't even manage to finish the question since the last word stuck in my throat like the fifth cracker swallowed without a sip of water in between.

Rather than answering immediately, Elle glanced at me sideways, the dark, empty highway giving her leeway to divide her attention as she drove. "Do you want to?"

Yes, of course I did. I didn't want to spend the rest of my life getting used to this pain, nor did I want to subject Gunner to the same agony.

And yet, the word that came out of my mouth—this time crackerless and adamant—was: "No."

"There's your answer."

For another half hour, the car rolled down the highway in silence, road noise dulled by the cocoon of comfort Gunner had paid top dollar for. Eventually, the warmth of the leather started feeling like Gunner's body spooning me. And I was halfway asleep when his half-sister spoke once again.

"Maybe we can come up with a compromise before we get there. You and Kira dividing your time between your grand-mother's estate and Atwood clan central. Or we could find something else the old woman covets...."

"Elle, stop it." She meant well, but every time I was remind-ed of my situation another wave of pain racked my body. And now I was starting to wonder whether my friend would be-tray my location after she returned with Kira, giving Gunner a roadmap to walk straight into a powerful kitsune's lair.

That couldn't happen. I could leave him—just barely. But I couldn't be responsible for further injury or death. "You have to promise not to tell your brother—either brother—where I'm going," I demanded, my voice so harsh Yuki turned over on the back seat.

"What if...?" Elle started.

But I shushed her in the werewolf way, with a hand laid gently on her forearm. "Elle, *promise*."

And, after one long moment of silence, my friend agreed.

WE WERE FIVE MINUTES tardy when the gate opened up before us despite there being no human operator visible. Snow had melted off the road, so the approach to Sakurako's mansion was easy to navigate. Within moments, Elle had pulled up beside the multi-colored fountain, then she and I glanced at each other in a sudden unity of thought.

We did not want to get out of that car.

Yuki, on the other hand, was glad to return to his mistress. He opened the back door with alacrity...and before any of us knew what was happening, Oyo had slipped between his legs and escaped.

"Grab her!" I yelled, scrambling to follow my own order. Without the fox, I had nothing to trade for Kira. And despite Oyo's leash spinning out behind her, we three resembled a circus act as we futilely tumbled over each other in the haste of our pursuit.

Only our clownishness was irrelevant because...

"Going somewhere?"

The elderly kitsune appeared out of nowhere inches in front of Oyo's nose. How had I ever thought of Sakurako as a little old lady? Now she towered above her former apprentice, magic buzzing like insects as Oyo's feet literally froze to the ground.

The four-legger yelped as she tried—and failed—to free them. But Sakurako's attention had already moved on to spear me as I pulled myself up out of the slush pile that seemed to have been placed there for the sole purpose of soaking my clothes.

"And *you*," she continued. "*You* are late."

"Where's Kira?" With an effort, I ignored the electricity seeping out of the pores of the other kitsune and headed toward the open front door instead. I hadn't missed the deadline by enough minutes that Kira should have suffered for it. But her absence was telling, to say the least.

Only my sister wasn't being punished for my lapses. Because even as I brushed past Sakurako, Kira was stepping out into the sunlight with a big smile on her face. "Mai! I've been waiting for you. I want to show you the library and..."

And no one had told the thirteen-year-old about the swap. Now it was my turn to glare at Sakurako, and I thought she might have actually wilted slightly beneath the force of my rage.

"Kira, walk with me," I interjected, taking my sister's hand for what was likely to be the last time in decades or at least years. The ache of my mate bond had dulled with distance, but now the pounding in my head leapt back to life with a jolt.

In response, my feet tried to stumble, but I pushed aside physical ailments and made my sister the entirety of my world for one brief moment. Still, she noticed my trembling, glanced back over one shoulder, asked me, "What's wrong?"

Rather than answering, I picked up the pace, surprised to find no complaint from my sister as she trotted right alongside me. Only when we were far enough away from our audience so shifter ears couldn't pick up on our conversation did we turn and face each other, neither of us initiating the movement but our toe tips meeting at the exact same time.

This was what we were losing. Sisterhood. Bonds of blood that ran deeper than mere genetics. I would never watch Kira blossom into womanhood, would never teach her to fight with a sharp-edged sword.

"You're going and I'm staying," I started. Then, as bargains and complaints rose in my sister's eyes, I shut her down abruptly. "I can't change this, Kira. Please don't ask me to."

Given the way she liked to gripe about everything from breakfast to homework, I thought she'd argue or at least rail against the fates and the world. Instead, my little sister stood as tall and straight as I did, asked a single question: "Until when?"

"I don't know," I told her truthfully. But, as Kira slipped cold fingers around my waist and hugged me tight enough to last a lifetime, I had a sinking suspicion our separation would last for a long, long time.

Chapter 37

Without Kira and Curly to guard from danger, I slept in the bed. Assuming, that is, the hours of tossing and turning could really be called sleep. Eventually, though, the sun rose and I groggily sat up to greet the daylight...only to be met by an agonizing burning where the mate tether intersected with my gut.

"Stay away. Stay safe," I whispered, barely able to speak over the spears of pain piercing my center. I knew I was too distant for my words to be captured by their intended recipient, but I *had* to try to keep Gunner in clan central. All it would take was one wave of Sakurako's fingers and he'd turn into a blood donor fueling who knew what kitsune atrocities at her whim.

And perhaps my request made it through after all. More likely, my body simply couldn't sustain that level of pain indefinitely. Whatever the reason, the throbbing receded to a dull ache after only a few seconds, and I sank back down into the soft mattress, pulling the comforter up over my head.

I lay there for minutes or hours, stroking the tendril of magic that connected me to my absent mate. The tether curled like a kitten around my fingers, warmed when I touched it...then surged back into piercing torment as the covers were ripped off from over my head.

"You've wallowed enough."

My grandmother stood above me, fully dressed and redolent with magic. When had I started smelling and seeing the influx of power as it gently seeped into her wrinkled skin? Whatever the reason behind my newfound abilities, the old woman now appeared spider-like, the only difference being that she consumed rather than spun her own web.

"Are you sick of tormenting Oyo already?" I muttered, turning over and trying to bury my face in one of the half dozen pillows arrayed across the bed between us. Then that soft cushion was yanked out from under me and I found myself tumbling over to land on my butt on the cold, hard floor.

"Oyo is immaterial," Sakurako answered. Then, raising one eyebrow, she offered information I hadn't asked for. "A golden collar isn't temporary, granddaughter. Oyo will remain a fox forever. I've sent her out into the forest to live as she wills."

Harsh. But perhaps kinder than the fate I'd thought the redheaded kitsune would be faced with. How would Sakurako punish my sister if I similarly failed to obey her commands?

The reminder of why I was here had me on my feet before Sakurako could prod me further. "What did you have in mind for today?" I asked even though I didn't really care how my apprenticeship started.

But Sakurako took my words at face value. "We are twenty years behind in your training, granddaughter," the old woman answered. "Today we will begin to remedy that mistake."

WE RECONVENED IN MY grandmother's study, a room decorated with reds and yellows and further warmed by a raging fireplace. Despite the moderate temperatures, however, I couldn't stop shivering as I huddled beneath a vast lap robe.

"Lighting a candle is the simplest example of pure magic," Sakurako explained, creating flame on all ten wicks simultaneously without expending any apparent effort at all. The candles flickered out, then she turned to face me. "Now you try."

I didn't want to, but this was what I'd signed up for. Learning to harness my kitsune nature and becoming my grandmother's mini-me. Ignoring the stab of complaint where my mate tether circled around my belly, I pulled up my star ball...then drew a blank.

Because—beyond blood magic, which was currently unavailable to me—the only thing I knew how to do was to physically toss my star ball at the candles and hope it sparked one of them on fire. But even I knew that was a terrible idea when loss of my magic made me droop and my hands were already shaking with a combination of exhaustion and cold.

Then Sakurako's fingers covered mine, her flesh warmer than expected as she pushed the star ball back inside my skin. "Not like that, granddaughter. You can't waste your own energy so flagrantly. You need to send out magic you've sucked in."

My head was pounding so hard it was difficult to focus. But I squinted against the pain and forced myself to pay attention as my grandmother lit the candles a second time. Ah, now I saw what she was doing. Saw the surge of power flowing from elsewhere—from her honor guard?—into her chest then back out through her fingers, igniting into flame.

Yuck. My grandmother was an energy vampire. And Sakurako must have understood my thought processes because she narrowed her eyes as she spoke.

"This is your heritage, granddaughter. A kitsune mistress gains the admiration of her honor guard then she uses that freely given power to protect them in exchange. It's an equal trade of energy, not so much different from what happens within a werewolf pack."

It was different. It was a whole-nother-ballpark different. Even as I assured myself of that fact, I stroked the tiny mating tendril still twined around my waist.

"Don't waste the werewolf for practice." I hadn't spoken a word since entering her study, but Sakurako carried on a conversation as if oblivious to that fact. "That bond is your most powerful source of energy. Save it for a rainy day."

"I won't use Gunner's affection. Rainy day or any day." My voice cracked as I spoke but I was no less adamant for the show of weakness.

"Then you'd better get to work on that honor guard, hadn't you?" Sakurako countered. "The most expedient path is getting hot and sweaty together. Just remember what I told you about showing favoritism at such an early date."

Chapter 38

The members of Sakurako's honor guard lived in their own wing on the first story of the mansion, behind a long line of doors with no identifying features to hint at who slept within. Given no way of guessing who was in residence at the moment, I banged on the first six doors one after another, then stood back as sleepy males stumbled out in pajamas, boxers, or in one case entirely nude.

"Um." I looked them over, noted that my grandmother had *definitely* included physique in her requirements for service. Then my gaze caught on Yuki at the end of the line.

Oyo's former lover appeared delighted to see me, despite the fact that he must have been on the night shift like the others. And yet, his presence sent a queasy rumbling through my gut.

"Yuki, go back to bed." Turning away so I wouldn't have to see the light in his eyes fade into disappointment, I addressed the other five men with more warmth in my tone. "I'd like to get to know you all better." Then I dropped my hand down to the sword belted at my hip, raised my eyebrows, and waited for them to catch on.

Then waited. And waited. For warriors, they were remarkably slow to get the message. Perhaps binding yourself to a kitsune mistress had a dulling effect on the mind?

Whatever the reason, all five of them just stood there awaiting further instructions. So, at last, I sighed then elaborated. "Get dressed and show me where you keep your swords. We're going to spar."

And *that* got them moving like I'd kicked over a hornet's nest.

I'D EXPECTED THERE to be a practice hall inside the mansion. But, instead, my five chosen warriors led me out the back and into a courtyard where flowering vines dripped and rotted off the rock walls and onto the ground. This was the result of kitsune magic, brilliant autumnal foliage killed before its proper hour by an unseasonal snow. Ignoring the shiver that passed through me at the realization, I split us up into three duos then proceeded to fight.

We were practicing rather than engaging in true battle, but we still used real weapons rather than padded blades. "I'm Koki," offered my opponent even as he dipped beneath my guard and nearly sliced through my jugular, the sun glinting brilliantly off his sword.

Rather than answering audibly, my blade deflected his and twisted sideways to slice at his exposed fingers as a retaliatory measure. He grinned as he danced backwards, sword flying so rapidly it turned into a blur before my eyes.

It was a pleasure to spar with a well-matched partner, even when he lunged nearly horizontally and managed to slice a thin nick in the only pair of jeans I now had to my name. I took advantage of the resistance of the fabric, however, and managed to cut the thinnest scratch across his forearm even as I told him, "I'm Mai."

Instantly, my opponent was bowing, speaking acknowledgement of my success directly to the ground. "I know who you are, Mai-sama. It is a great honor to lose to you."

I smiled...and that's when it happened. A streak of magic arced like lightning away from his groin and into my center. It was lewd and unpleasant...and infused me with so much energy I thought I might have been able to levitate into open air.

"SWITCH PARTNERS!" MY voice came out high and breathy, an almost orgasmic pleasure suffusing my core. I'd thought I was so clever choosing swordplay rather than bedplay...and yet it appeared the results were largely the same.

But I grimaced and bore it. Learned names and fighting habits of four other devotees then gritted my teeth as, one after another, magical connections formed between me and the humans I crossed swords with. Only when the fifth tether threatened to dislodge my older connection to Gunner did I bend over gasping, drawing the concerned attention of the rest of the honor guard.

"What did you do to her?" Koki demanded. "We allow the mistress to win always!"

They hadn't even been fighting to the full extent of their prowess? Grabbing Gunner's tether in one fist so it couldn't escape me, I didn't bother to dismiss them. Just stormed out of the training yard and back into the mansion from which we'd come.

Up the stairs, down a hallway, into the study where Saku-rako had recently prodded me with beginner magic. My neme-sis sat behind her desk with a book open before her, not both-ering to glance up when I pushed my way inside the room.

"Done already?" she asked after a moment of silence. Or not silence, but the harsh sound of me panting as I strained to cling to a slippery mate bond that kept trying to slide out of my grasp.

Later, I'd wonder why I didn't release the connection. Why I didn't break the bond between me and Gunner and put us both out of our misery. In the moment, however, I merely de-manded, "Put my mate bond back."

"*I* didn't dislodge it. And *I* can't replace it." Despite the quietness of her words, Sakurako deigned to place one finger on the page to hold her place before looking up from her book. Her eyes had all the warmth of hard nubs of coal stuck in a snowman's head.

"So how do *I* fix it?" I growled, sounding an awful lot like a werewolf. And I was somehow unsurprised when the old woman raised her left hand and gestured at the candelabra I'd failed to light earlier in the day.

Yes, that was right. I felt like I'd eaten too much, like the last bite of dessert was hovering halfway down my throat want-ing to come back up as vomit. The obvious answer was to bleed off some of the excess magic and hope my connection to Gun-ner would snap back into place once given sufficient room.

So I focused all of my anger on those unlit wicks, expecting the process to be time-consuming and difficult. But, instead, I merely opened my mouth and breathed toward the candles...then watched wax puddle on the tabletop as the entire candelabra went up in a massive blaze.

"Control will be next on our agenda," Sakurako noted dryly, dropping her head back down to the book she'd been reading. But I caught a faint hint of a smile ghosting across her features and her eyes didn't slide back and forth across the page.

My grandmother was proud of my first attempt at pure kitsune magic. A week ago, such familial pride would have warmed the sodden lump in my stomach and threatened to create a full-on thaw.

Now, though, I had interest in nothing other than the way Gunner's mate bond wove itself amidst the honor guard's tethers as it was cemented back into my stomach. *That* connection was now solid and immovable, exactly what I'd been aiming for.

So why did I feel profoundly disloyal as I turned my back on my grandmother and took my leave?

Chapter 39

"*S*tay away. *Stay safe.*" I spoke before I'd fully woken, a dream of Sakurako stealing my tether and using Gunner as a blood slave sending me fumbling for the light. Only after I stared down at my stomach and easily picked out my mate bond did I relax my muscles. Two of the human males' tethers had sloughed off during the intervening hours, but Gunner's had burrowed deeper down into my flesh and stuck.

Being able to physically see a connection that pulsed beneath the skin of my belly should have been disconcerting. But, instead, I stroked the tether gently while straining—and failing—to feel the werewolf on the other end of the line.

Nothing.

Closing my eyes, I reminded myself that Gunner was there even if I couldn't communicate with him. Still, he was also at risk due to my proximity to Sakurako. I pursed my lips, fully aware that the smart solution involved breaking our mate bond immediately. But, instead, I resolved to find a way to maintain our connection without risking my werewolf partner to Sakurako's wrath.

A seemingly impossible task...so I'd better get right on it. Even though it wasn't yet dawn, I pulled on clothes and padded out into the hallway. *The library.* Kira had emoted over that room before I'd told her she was leaving, and it seemed like the obvious place to start.

Light was beginning to filter in various windows by the time I'd peeked into ballrooms and kitchens and guest rooms before finally arrowing in on my goal. But then I stood gaping in the doorway rather than getting right to work.

There were so many books. Hundreds of them, thousands of them, spines spanning every inch from vaulted ceiling to tiled floor. This collection bore no resemblance to the few, handwritten journal entries Elle had found during the summer we spent sussing out my abilities. Instead, as I slipped book after book from the shelves, flipping through pages full of fox shifters and magic, I knew I'd struck the mother lode.

The question was—how to find a needle in this tremendous haystack? The only solution appeared to be to read. Which is exactly how Sakurako found me three hours later, my nose in the tenth or perhaps twentieth musty old book.

"Looking for something?"

I jumped at her question, slammed the cover shut so quickly I nearly took off my own hand. Then the book was being yanked out of my possession by impatient fingers, the same pages fluttering open as my hostess pored over the title page.

"*Kitsune History for Beginners.*" Sakurako raised one eyebrow. "Very basic information, granddaughter."

"In case you weren't aware, that's the level I'm currently at."

We watched each other in silence for one long moment before a hint of softness rose behind the old woman's eyes. "Your mother was equally willing to admit to weakness. It's a surprisingly useful trait."

She graced me with that same smile of a proud teacher I'd seen on her features earlier. And to my disgust, a cloud of confused acceptance promptly roiled through my gut.

WE SETTLED INTO A PREDICTABLE rhythm thereafter. Mornings were for reading and practicing. Afternoons were for building bonds with my honor guard. Every day, I woke with a plea on my lips— *"Stay away. Stay safe."* And every night, I fell into an exhausted slumber, alone in my solitary bed.

"When will it be my turn to spar again?" Koki asked me a week—nine days?—later when we passed each other in the hall. He must have rotated off night shift because it was just after lunchtime, yet he appeared unusually bright-eyed and bushy-tailed.

"You cheat. It's no fun to fight a cheater." I tried to glower at the human, but he was too perkily cheerful to serve as the focus of my ire. The last time we'd sparred together, I'd been sure he was actually struggling flat out against me...until I'd slipped on a patch of mud and still managed to come out ahead.

"Mai-sama, losing to you is such supreme pleasure. Why would I want to win?" As he spoke, the human raised my hand to his lips, eyes not flickering away from mine for even a second. And, in response, the surge of energy along our shared tether transitioned from a trickle into a flood.

"I haven't sparred with everyone yet," I protested. "It's not fair to fight against you a third time until everyone else has had a shot." As I spoke, I removed my hand from his and averted my own gaze while butterflies danced in my belly. It was painfully difficult in that moment to remember the shape of Gunner's face.

"Not true," Koki countered and began spouting off semi-familiar names. I counted on my fingers as he listed his compatriots, then I nodded definitively when he came to the end.

"That's seventeen," I agreed. "But there are eighteen doors in the honor-guard hallway."

And, for the first time in our acquaintance, Koki turned evasive. "Mai-sama, perhaps now is not the time to…"

"The eighteenth door is locked. I tried it yesterday. I want to know what—or who—is inside."

"Mai-chan." The endearment wasn't entirely unexpected, but it nonetheless raised a knot in my throat I couldn't quite decipher. "Please believe me. You don't want this."

"I do want this. Do you have the key or should I ask my grandmother?"

Our standoff lasted for nearly thirty seconds before Koki caved beneath my stubbornness. He was the unofficial leader of the honor guard and we both knew it. Of course he possessed the requested key.

So, silently, we descended to the ground-floor level. Koki reluctantly trailed me down the hallway before slipping a thin chain off over his head once we reached the end. The silver key waited there between us, Koki's mouth compressing with the effort to restrain the warning on the tip of his tongue.

I accepted the key but not the warning, noted how the metal was hot against my fingers while the doorknob was cold against my skin. I was suddenly unsure whether I did want to uncover this secret. And Koki confirmed that fact as his fingers drifted reassuringly across the back of my neck.

"What you have to understand, Mai-sama, is that any of us would willingly sacrifice ourselves for the sake of the mistress. Kaito volunteered to help Sakurako-sama punish the wrongdo-er and was chosen above all of us for his strength and loyalty. I also requested the honor, many of us requested the honor, and Kaito would do it all over again."

The door swung open as I struggled—and failed—to come up with an answer to that expression of extreme fidelity. And what I saw inside wasn't as terrible as I'd been led to expect.

In the room, IVs trailed from a strange male's body as he lay unmoving on a hospital bed. His chest rose and fell with regularity, but I didn't see so much as an eyelash-flicker of voluntary movement in response to our presence or to Koki's voice.

This wasn't a monster, but simply a man in a coma. The monster lay elsewhere in the mansion, far above this formerly locked room.

Chapter 40

"**Y**ou're going to *fix* this."

I slammed into Sakurako's study in a high temper. And when the old woman tried to hide behind her book this time, I ripped the object out of her hands and flung it across the room. Elle would have been horrified at the way the book landed spine up, pages crumpling beneath the cover. But I was grimly satisfied to have broken something that didn't live and breathe.

"So you found Kaito."

"Is that your only answer? About a man who can't even feed himself, who just lies there staring at the ceiling with no life force left for you to harvest?"

I wasn't actually asking, but Sakurako answered anyway. "Yes. It was a shame, but necessary. And, no, it cannot be fixed."

Necessary. Sakurako's cold acceptance of her underling's vegetative state forced the air out of my lungs and I found myself sinking into the nearest armchair. My own rage was abruptly extinguished, the future yawning out before me like a dark tunnel with no end.

This is what I'd signed on for when I traded my future for Kira's. I had no grounds for complaint when I'd offered myself up as Sakurako's apprentice without requiring a single reassurance on her part.

And Sakurako must have smelled the regret I drowned in because her voice gentled when she spoke to me. "Granddaughter," the old woman said quietly. Then, when I failed to respond, her voice sharpened. "You will *not* be as weak as your mother. If you can't handle the truth, then I will train your sister instead."

"We had a deal." Now the fire was back in my veins and I had to cling to my temper to prevent myself from leaping across the desk and strangling the old woman.

"We did. And if you don't hold up your end of the bargain then I see no reason to hold up mine."

My magic was a mere pinprick compared to my grandmother's, but for one split second I considered blasting her with everything I had and hoping it would wipe her off the face of the earth. But the likelihood of failure rose before me along with the specter of Kira's lost innocence. So I forced my voice to harden as I returned to business instead.

"I'm here, aren't I? And I understand that Oyo needed to be prevented from continuing what she was doing. But couldn't you have harvested a little bit of energy from each member of your honor guard rather than draining Kaito dry? Can't you push power back into him from his friends?"

Now I was just grasping at straws, but Sakurako provided me more leeway than I'd expected. She sighed, and for a second I thought she might regret her own actions. "That's not how big magic works," she started. Then her subsequent words turned that supposed empathy into a lie. "Kaito's life is a small price to pay for keeping the werewolf packs from restarting their vendetta against all kitsunes. The sacrifice was necessary and I'd do it again tomorrow. When the time comes, so will you."

No. Just—*no*. I refused to accept that the ends justified the means when it came to stealing the life of an innocent. I refused to think that Sakurako would expect me to take part in similar atrocities as my own magic grew.

All I managed to say aloud, however, was: "That's inhuman."

"Yes, it is, granddaughter. Because we aren't humans; neither one of us is. Instead, we are kitsunes. And expedience is what we do best."

I TORE THE LIBRARY apart in search of another solution. There had to be a way to embrace my heritage that didn't involve vampiric energy harvests and questionable moral choices.

But there were so many books and they were all so disorganized. It seemed highly unlikely I'd find the answer in a single night.

Still, I gritted my teeth and dipped into histories of kitsune lineages, lesson plans for advanced magical techniques, and picture books clearly intended for soon-to-be foxes. All the while, Gunner's tether twisted and tugged at my stomach, like a bloodling puppy who didn't understand why he was being ignored.

"There has to be a compromise," I murmured, laughing grimly as I realized how closely my words mirrored Elle's sentiments when I chose to leave Gunner behind. She'd been wrong then and I was wrong now...and yet I still had to try.

So I read and skimmed and climbed tall ladders searching through books on the upper levels. And sometime long after midnight I must have fallen asleep in the midst of my research because gnarled fingers once again shook me awake.

"Stay…" I started my morning mantra, only to be interrupted by Sakurako's belated explanation for Kaito's fate and my own apprenticeship.

"My child, I do this to protect you." Her voice was scratchy, reluctant, as if she expected to be rebuffed before she finished what she'd come here to say. "I wish I'd done the same for your mother. It's my own fault that she's dead."

And something about the older woman's admission made me want to wrap her up in a blanket and hug her to my chest. This was, after all, the mother of my mother. My own flesh and blood.

"Sobo," I murmured, using the pet name I hadn't even thought since being blackmailed into trading places with my sister.

"Granddaughter," she answered, her bones creaking as she lowered herself down onto the ottoman on which my feet rested. "This is a difficult situation for both of us. But please know how glad I am to have you here beside me. It's a lonely life, being a kitsune. Less lonely since you arrived to make my house into a home."

I was still half asleep, but in that moment I could imagine Sakurako as a young woman. Could guess how her own mother or grandmother had indoctrinated her into their beliefs, how she'd had no more choice coming to terms with her heritage than I did with mine.

If I stayed on my current road, someday I'd do the same thing to my own daughter or granddaughter. Someday I'd rip the rug out from under my offspring's feet and watch innocence fade from her dark-irised eyes.

Then this hypothetical descendant would repeat the maneuver for the sake of her own daughter or granddaughter. And on and on the wheel would turn until it was sad-eyed foxes all the way down.

Which is why I did it. Used the information discovered in the hundredth book but rejected as too awful to contemplate.

Scrabbled at my waist without looking downward and yanked at the first tether my fingers came in contact with.

Materialized a shard of pure magic...then thrust that disloyal dagger directly into my grandmother's heaving breast.

Chapter 41

Did I steal the life force from Gunner?

I was wide awake the moment the thought struck me. Ignoring the brilliant flare of magic surrounding my grandmother, I instead frantically felt at my stomach in search of my mate bond.

Surely I would have known if the magic beneath my fingers belonged to a werewolf instead of to a human. The odds were seventeen to one against, and yet....

Gunner's tether was the one I stroked when I felt lonely. Gunner's tether was the one that rose to my fingers like an affectionate cat. Would his tether also be the one that responded to my frantic need unbidden? Would he throw himself into the void with the same loyalty as a member of Sakurako's honor guard?

Unfortunately, stolen magic flared and buzzed all around me. I couldn't for the life of me tell whether the missing tether belonged to an alpha werewolf.

Meanwhile, Sakurako was slowing her own transition even as magic twined into a collar around her neck just as it had done around Oyo's. "I'm proud of you," she whispered, fighting the magic...and failing to escape just as the book had said she would.

Because, although powerful, this magic was seductively simple. Or so the book had promised. I couldn't have gotten it wrong when the recipe included only three parts.

Use every ounce of magic embodied by a loyal underling. Strike in a moment of trust and shared understanding. Watch your loved one turn into a fox with no possibility of ever coming back.

The book hadn't mentioned how my eyes would fill with water, tears making it impossible to figure out whose tether I'd stolen even as my grandmother was forced out of her human skin forever. "Sobo," I murmured. "I'm sorry."

"Never apologize for the necessary, granddaughter."

And then she was my grandmother no longer. Instead, sharp, dark eyes met mine from within the face of a fox.

Only this was a subtly different fox than the one I'd fled beside when racing away from Atwood clan central. Sakurako then had been snow-white and nine-tailed. Now, her fur was speckled with gray and she possessed only one tail.

In other words, she looked like a wild animal, not a fox-form kitsune. Still, she maintained the same lithe fluidity as she leapt from chair to floor to window ledge. Her collar gleamed golden, then she was outside in the early morning. Was sprinting for distant trees as a herd of bare feet heralded her honor guard racing into the library to lend their mistress aid.

Or, rather, to lend their *new* mistress aid. "Mai-sama. I knew you would be triumphant." This was Koki, kneeling at my feet, his hand on my knee even as his tether refilled the empty reservoir of magic inside me. The surge of power was heady and riveting...and gave me a nearly uncontrollable urge to throw up.

But then my gorge calmed as I noted my mate bond springing back into existence at the same moment. I hadn't turned the vibrant alpha into a vegetable after all. And for at least a minute, I didn't care whose life I'd ruined in his place.

"HE WILL BE TAKEN CARE of Mai-sama."

We stood around the bed of the male whose life I'd stolen for the sake of my own freedom. And I hated the fact that I couldn't remember his name, couldn't recall the sleeper's signature fencing move nor bring to mind a single identifying feature that set him apart from all of the other humans squeezed into the small space that made up his sickroom.

But that wasn't the point. The point—after the better part of a day spent poring over Sakurako's finances—was dealing with responsibilities that were now my own. As my grandmother's sole heir, I would inherit her extravagant wealth and numerous properties. I planned to use both to ensure these males who had sacrificed so much for the sake of a kitsune mistress could now live simple human lives.

The first step in achieving that goal was breaking the bonds that bound them so they could figure out their own paths into the future. So I raised my voice and spoke to the assemblage. "I appreciate your service. But you are now dismissed."

Magic bit into my waist as one tether snapped and sprang away from me, then someone in the back turned and left the sickroom. Yuki. Gone to seek out his fox-form lover? Everyone else, however, stood their ground and stared at me as if I was speaking Portuguese.

"You can go out into the world. Take whatever you want from the mansion. Use Sakurako's money to live on. But make your own lives. Be free." As I spoke, I tried to push past the nearest humans to follow Yuki, but I found myself blocked at every turn.

"We don't want to be free, Mai-sama." This was Koki, speaking for the remaining fifteen humans. "You are the new mistress. We will stay here beside you. Or go anywhere you wish to wander. We are your honor guard."

"No, you're not." My face was hot, and I suddenly felt trapped in the midst of the assembled humans. Would I be forced to fight my way free due to my own manipulations? Sakurako would be laughing up her sleeve if she hadn't fled so preemptively into the cold.

"It's all we know, Mai-sama," Koki said.

"Yes, it is our honor and our duty to serve you," offered another voice. Then the same sentiment in multiple different incarnations rose to fill the room.

So I did the only thing I could think of—I chose my own selfishness over extended explanations. Donning the form of my fox, I grabbed tethers in my teeth one after another and gnawed through every one of them until I was one bond away from entirely free.

Because these men might think they wanted to be my honor guard. But they couldn't think, not really, not with my kitsune nature skimming off the cream of their energy.

In time, I suspected they'd come to their senses. But, for now, there was only one place I wanted to be...and it certainly wasn't here.

So I gnawed until magic flung itself away from me like broken rubber bands, knocking male after male down into a tumble of bellows and elbows. And I was as heartless as my grandmother because I didn't care about their pain or confusion. All I cared about was the single tether remaining. The one thick rope of glowing magic leading me out of the mansion toward the west.

I'd been separated from my mate for far too long already. With a mental promise to reassess my responsibilities in the near future, I took to my heels and I ran.

Chapter 42

Returning to fox form after days spent entirely human should have come as a relief, even more so when I was finally traveling toward my absent mate. But the tethers of my honor guards snapped back into place before I'd gone half a mile, and I ended up slogging slowly through a sodden landscape rather than dancing fleet-footed toward the west.

Still, I was single-mindedly adamant about pushing onward. Even after rational sense reasserted itself and told me that I'd get to Gunner faster if I retreated to the mansion, used Sakurako's telephone, and called a cab.

Instead, I fought against the magical headwind, pausing only when I reached a vast pool of water that cut me off from running straight toward Gunner. Right or left? Either direction made my stomach equally queasy. And as I racked my brain, trying to remember which route Elle had used to drive here, my attention caught on the reflection in the lake that blocked my path.

I was as familiar with my fox form as I was with my human one. Red fur, white-tipped tail, black nose and paws. But that wasn't the sight that greeted me in the water. Instead, my pelt had turned so white I might as well have been albino, although my eyes still gleamed black on either side of my head.

I spun in a circle, trying to catch sight of the other obvious visual difference between myself and my grandmother. As best I could tell, I still had only one tail....

And even though the change in coloration—and the change in self it likely represented—was disconcerting, the spinning action managed to unstick my latent sense of direction. *Left.* I was somehow positive that was the direction closest to Gunner. So I shook off the surprise of being bleached white in an instant and followed the lakeshore south even as the sun sank down toward the west.

I'd be spending the night outside in fur form if I didn't achieve civilization quickly, which would be annoying given the muddy soil and the lack of dry leaves to nest within. Still it was impatience rather than discomfort that hastened my footsteps. I *needed* to see Gunner so badly the wish had turned into a physical ache.

Tethers still streamed behind me like anchors. But they were weaker than they had been earlier, less likely to make me stumble and fall. So I picked up the pace and was running headlong when I felt my nails clicking against pavement after topping a short rise.

A road. And this time my tether informed me to turn right instead of left.

Only...there were headlights approaching from that direction. Headlights that materialized into a strangely familiar vehicle—Old Red screeching to a halt.

I leapt upward into humanity as Gunner emerged and raced toward me. I grabbed my mate and clung tightly even as he lifted me off my feet and spun me in a circle as if he was searching for my human tail.

"I love you." I laughed into the wind of our passing before adding: "But you know that already. Because you came for me."

His answer made me laugh harder despite the growly undertones. "I would have been here a week earlier if you hadn't kept telling me to stay away."

His mouth covered mine for one long, hard moment. Then he separated us long enough to demand precisely what I longed to give him. "I won't push you to change and you won't keep me out of your life any longer."

"Of course not," I told my forever mate.

OUR ROAD TRIP HOME was slow and meandering, but not because of Old Red's infirmities. While I was gone, Gunner had not only reclaimed my beloved vehicle, he'd also totally replaced everything underneath the hood.

"So, really, she's not Old Red any longer," I teased as we got back into the car after stopping for ice cream only a few miles out from clan central. There had been various other treats during the intervening twenty-four hours, the ones in our hotel room largely responsible for the huge grin currently plastered across my face.

"I didn't replace the car's body or the interior," Gunner countered, his hands intertwining with mine atop the center console as if the sixty seconds we'd been separated to get into our respective seats had lasted far too long. My favorite alpha was physically healed but still had a hard time letting a moment pass without touching me. Luckily, that wasn't a problem since I felt the exact same way.

"We could call her Not-so-old Red," I suggested. "Or Cinnamon Rocket." There was some serious horsepower now when I punched down on the gas pedal.

"Or Safer Rustbucket," Gunner countered even as we turned onto the driveway for clan central and rolled toward the main street.

After that, we fell silent as I remembered that I wouldn't be sneaking into a cottage on the periphery of the werewolf settlement this time. Kira had made that decision while I was absent, informing me over the phone that Gunner's addition "is way too cool to leave while you get your panties out of their twist and accept the good thing knocking on you door."

Despite her mixed metaphors, I decided my sister was surprisingly wise, at least in this instance. As a result, I'd be moving in as the pack leader's mate today the way I should have done from the beginning. Smiling, I gave Gunner's hand a squeeze.

Intention was powerful among werewolves, so I wasn't surprised that bonds zapped toward me out of nowhere as I maneuvered Old Red down the narrow street that bisected clan central. Still, I flinched when the first returning tether struck my stomach, then I held my breath and waited for the strangely orgasmic reaction that had resulted from building connections with Sakurako's honor guard.

Instead, only a faint hint of warmth infused my belly. And shifter neighbors nodded easy greetings without seeming unduly affected by our presence as we rolled past.

Okay, now I was curious. Given our speed of under ten miles per hour combined with an arrow-straight trajectory, I didn't hesitate to take my hand off the wheel and tug at one of the stronger bonds connecting me to Gunner's pack mates.

Were Atwood shifters feeding me magic the way Sakurako's honor guard had, or did the power flow the other way?

"Stop!"

Gunner's hand spun the wheel sideways even as I slammed on the brakes. And it was a good thing he'd replaced the pads and rotors or I would have struck the bloodling puppy who'd responded to my summoning by launching himself directly into our path.

"Curly!" I threw the car into park and leapt out of the vehicle, knowing I hadn't hit the youngster but still worried he'd somehow gotten hurt in the process. And as I did so, I could feel my own energy streaming down the tether, perking up Curly's ears and making him prance with delight.

So this was what a werewolf connection looked like. Energy flowing freely in both directions, from the stronger shifter to wherever it was needed most. This was as different from a kitsune's tether as day was from night.

And for the first time in over a week, my shoulders relaxed fully. Because, yes, I'd made terrible mistakes getting here. I hadn't been fast enough or smart enough to save Edward. I'd stolen the humanity from Oyo and from my own grandmother. And I'd thoroughly shaken up the Atwood pack.

But, despite literally changing my skin while denning with my grandmother, Curly recognized me as the same person who had left here a little over a week before. Plus, what I lacked in kitsune power, I now made up for with the wealth of a werewolf pack.

And, apparently, the shifters around me were glad to have me present. Because tethers arrowed in one after another, weaving themselves together like a blanket enfolding my body until it seemed not a single additional tether would fit.

Only there was room for one more after all, as I discovered when the werewolf gossip tree propagated further. There was always room for one more.

Curly, bored by self realization, reared up on his hind legs to claw at my kneecaps, and I answered by hoisting him into my arms. Then I leaned into Gunner—who, predictably, was right there behind me when I needed him. And I stated the obvious.

"It's good to be home."

Epilogue

"**N**o! Not the serrated knife!" As I watched, Becky yanked the utensil in question out of the hand of an inept male werewolf. "Use *this* one to slice carrots."

I couldn't help smiling at the formerly quiet werewolf's bossiness, and even more so at the way her student obeyed immediately with no biting commentary about the bloodling puppy frolicking at their feet. Six weeks after my return, the pack was almost unrecognizable. Which wasn't to say the male werewolves had entirely come around.

For example, they'd nearly universally chosen the afternoon shift when presented with Thanksgiving-cooking choices. And I'd been dumb enough to let Gunner join the early-bird females while leaving the untrained werewolf males to me.

As a result of my lack of foresight, I'd been responsible for bandaging up the first chef wannabe who injured himself through improper use of kitchen equipment. And when a second male had accidentally-on-purpose sliced into the pad of his hand instead of into the potatoes he was supposedly peeling, I'd slapped rubber gloves over the shifter's bandage and started him on the huge pile of dishes in the sink rather than sending him home as he clearly wished.

Since then, the only injuries had been accidents. Which didn't mean there hadn't been dozens of them. Perhaps that explained the shiver of premonition that kept fluttering up my spine?

"Something wrong?" Elle diverted Curly before the pup could land in the vat of mashed potatoes, my friend's mere presence relaxing my shoulders down away from my ears. I'd sent a formal Thanksgiving invitation over to Ransom's territory two weeks earlier, but Elle was the only one who'd bothered showing up.

"I wish your brother was here," I told her honestly. "Your other brother, I mean."

"If Gunner had invited him, Ransom would have come," Elle answered carefully.

"I know." And I did.

Because—as much as I loved Gunner—I could admit that both brothers were equally bull-headed in their stubbornness. It was a wonder, really that they'd found a way to work together from a distance in the weeks since clan central had been invaded by neighboring wolves. On the plus side, the siblings' alliance meant the sentries patrolling our boundary were bored out of their skulls after weeks of searching without sighting a single intruder. I was apparently the only one who felt an empty space in the web of pack bonds where Ransom should have slotted in.

"Hey, this might make you feel better." Elle was a master at changing the subject so she didn't get caught in the middle between hard-headed half-brothers who still stubbornly refused to talk to each other. And her choice of topic sucked me in just as she'd known it would. "Koki left Sakurako's compound last week, and Haru checked out on Monday. Which only leaves five guys still there, plus the bedridden."

That *was* good news. And I was even more grateful to Elle for making weekly trips to work on my grandmother's library while also taking the slowly dwindling honor guard under her wing. I kept hoping she would find a way to break through whatever magic kept two of the males in a coma. But even if my grandmother was right and that damage turned out to be permanent, at least sixteen lives would have been saved from the vagaries of a kitsune's whim.

"Thank you," I started, smiling as I watched Curly dance up to a male who would have kicked the pup aside three months earlier. This time, the youngster ended up ensconced on the shifter's broad lap instead. Atwood pack bonds grew smoother and stronger every time I looked at them. What could be better than that?

Then the flutter of premonition that had been bothering me for hours turned into a spear of ice striking between my shoulder blades. I whirled, eyes scanning the assemblage even as the chatter of voices around us slowed then entirely faded away.

Because Elizabeth was standing in the doorway naked, one hand pressed into her side as if she'd run so fast she'd injured herself. "There are enemies at the border," she gasped out after a terrifying second.

Only, she was wrong, because I could hear wolves racing closer in the newfound silence. There weren't enemies at the border. There were enemies outside our door.

I REACHED DOWN AND yanked at the tethers twining around my waist as one unit, felt absent pack mates respond at once to the wordless summons I'd sent out. Meanwhile, I barked orders to the shifters present in the kitchen. "Get the elderly and children into attics." Wolves were bad at ladders and I had a feeling our invaders would stick, at least for a while, to fur and claws.

Then I was sprinting out the door to greet the enemy, my sword glowing and whistling through the air as I ran. Who would invade clan central on Thanksgiving? Unfortunately, only one alpha was aware of our plans down to the hour...and I'd been the stupid traitor who clued him in.

Sure enough, I recognized Ransom at the head of the wolves streaming toward me. There were dozens of them, more than had followed Ransom into exile, more than I'd seen on Kelleys Island, and definitely more than I had at my own back.

Meanwhile, their leader's scent was nothing like the Atwood ozone it had been when I first met him. Instead, Ransom now smelled like a thumbnail run across the skin of an unripe orange—bitter and sour and biting all at once.

"Find Gunner and..." I started. But then strong hands were pushing mc sideways. My mate was before me even as he dropped down into the form of his wolf.

So Gunner wasn't even going to try words first. I swallowed and forced myself not to gainsay him. This was what it meant to be the mate of an alpha—backing my partner up even when I thought he was wrong.

I expected Ransom's entire pack to surge forward and for the males behind me to shift and retaliate. But, instead, only the two alphas crashed together, the rest of us an avid audience to their heated attack.

"Should we…?" a male behind me started. But I held up one hand even though blood sprayed across the pavement, the pair of wolves moving too quickly for me to tell which one had gotten hurt.

Blood wasn't good…but it was still better than a full-clan pitched battle. So I clamped my hands down on the pack bonds that spiraled out away from me, forcing angry shifters to hold their tempers and stand their ground.

Whether Ransom would be able to do the same while tearing into his brother was another matter. But even as I eyed our opponents, the fighting wolves were wolves no longer. Instead, the brothers were human and naked, rolling across the pavement with Gunner's arm around Ransom's neck while Ransom's fist pounded into Gunner's gut.

"You're late," Gunner growled, releasing Ransom and surging upward, then reaching down to help his brother to his feet.

"I heard you were making everybody help with the cooking. So the way I see it, I'm right on time."

Wait. So this wasn't an invasion…it was guests arriving for Thanksgiving dinner?

As if he'd heard my question, Gunner glanced sideways, an eye that was already starting to swell and purple closing into the tiniest, subtlest wink. An alpha really did know everything that happened in his pack apparently…including his mate's illicit attempt to bring the prodigal brother back into the fold.

"Well, there's always dishwashing afterwards," Gunner said companionably. And as one unit, both Atwood alphas and every shifter they ruled over interwove seamlessly as they raced for the nearly completed Thanksgiving feast.

"Can you move any faster? I'm starving!" This was Kira, mini drama queen who had wisely joined Gunner for the earlier shift in the kitchen. Her tone was snarky, but I was beginning to speak teenager. This particular example meant, *"Thanks for finding such awesome werewolves to den with. And, by the way, let's eat."*

Behind her, Tank and Allen winked at me, then headed toward the long series of food-laden tables with Becky safely sandwiched in their midst. There were males and females, children and warriors all intermingled without regard for status within a single line.

And as I surveyed the crowd, I realized I had everything I'd ever wanted spread out before me. Mate, family, and a pack.

Well, almost everything I'd ever wanted. Because my sister had a point, as usual. Given the ferocity of werewolf appetites, I'd better hurry if I wanted to grab some pumpkin pie and stuffing before the best parts of the feast were gone.

From the Author

Thank you so much for joining Mai on her adventures! If you're not quite ready to say goodbye to this world of sword-wielding shifters, you can download bonus extras along with a free starter library if you sign up for my email list at www.aimeeeasterling.com.

Or dive straight into Terra's story with the free novel *Shiftless*. After years of suppressing her inner wolf, Terra struggles to forget her pack. But when her past finally comes calling, she has no choice but reclaim the predator within....

15278222R00132

Printed in Great Britain
by Amazon